泠崎踏歌

Singing Forward Despite Hardships

曾艳丽 ◎ 著

新华出版社

图书在版编目（CIP）数据

沧崎踏歌 / 曾艳丽著 . -- 北京 ： 新华出版社，
2021.11

ISBN 978-7-5166-6178-9

Ⅰ . ①沧… Ⅱ . ①曾… Ⅲ . ①诗集－中国－当代
Ⅳ . ① I227

中国版本图书馆 CIP 数据核字（2022）第 018757 号

沧崎踏歌

作　　者：曾艳丽

责任编辑：李　成
封面设计：树上微出版

出版发行：新华出版社
地　　址：北京石景山区京原路 8 号　　　　　　　**邮　　编：**100040
网　　址：http://www.xinhuapub.com　　http://www.xinhuanet.com
经　　销：新华书店
购书热线：010-63077122　　　　**中国新闻书店购书热线：**010-63072012

照　　排：树上微出版
印　　刷：湖北金港彩印有限公司
成品尺寸：142mm×210mm
印　　张：7.5　　　　　　　　**字　　数：**132 千字
版　　次：2022 年 2 月第一版　　　**印　　次：**2022 年 2 月第一次印刷
书　　号：ISBN 978-7-5166-6178-9
定　　价：98.00 元

作者简介

曾艳丽

　　笔名竹真，女，1981年2月出生，四川乐山人，中共党员，中国散文网会员，湖北省翻译协会会员，福建省普通话水平测试员。热爱校园，钟情文字，曾主持CCTV"希望之星"英语风采大赛襄樊赛区决赛，作品散见于《当代诗歌精选》《中华情全国诗歌散文集》《厦门日报》《集美校友》等，曾荣获"千禧杯"全国散文诗歌大奖赛三等奖、中国当代作家书画家代表作文库二等奖、湖北省外语口译大赛二等奖、福建省第二届中华经典诵读大赛教师组二等奖等奖项，参与编撰全国21世纪星火计划英语系列规划教材，现为集美大学管理干部。

目录

contents

第三篇章 校之纯美 梦之可期 / 071
Chapter Three The Beauty of School is Pure, the Dream is Worth Expecting

目
录

国之大
心之厦

Chapter One

The Brand Country,
the Depending Heart

祖国，您是我心底最坚强的温柔

我在泰山之巅凝望您
您的脸庞是那样端庄美丽
我深深知道
您曾经饱尝苦难与欺凌

我在北国冰雪中凝望您
您的眼神是那样刚毅坚定
我深深知道
您曾经在沧桑坎坷中艰难前行

我在江南小桥边凝望您
您的心跳是那样安详平静
我深深知道
您已将辛酸苦痛化作云淡风轻

我在东海之滨凝望您
您的胸怀是那样广博无际
我深深知道
您要让十四亿儿女相亲相依

我在大厦之顶凝望您
您的脉搏是那样青春有力
我深深知道
您正在为伟大的梦想朝夕奋进

祖国，每当想起您
心底是最深的眷恋与疼惜
您深潜海底的勇气与九天揽月的豪情
给我不竭的希冀与动力

亲爱的祖国
深深祝福您
有五十六个民族儿女齐心培育
您的梦想之花必将开遍神州华夏每一寸土地

My Motherland, You Are the Strongest Gentleness of My Heart

I gaze at you on the top of Mount Tai
Your face is so elegant and beautiful
I deeply know
You endured suffering and turmoil

I gaze at you in the snow and ice of the north
Your eyes are so firm and resolute
I deeply know
You have ever struggled in the vicissitudes

I gaze at you beside a bridge of Jiangnan
Your heart is so pulsing with serenity
I deeply know
You have turned the afflictions into prosperity

I gaze at you on the shore of the East China Sea

Your mind stretches to infinity

I deeply know

You want your 1.4 billion children to stand in unity

I gaze at you on the top of a building

Your pulse is full of youth and might

I deeply know

You are striving for the great dream day and night

My motherland, when I think of you

Suffusing my heart is the deepest attachment and love

Your courage and ambition to explore the universe

Give me endless hope and impetus

My dear motherland

Wish you all the best

Fifty-six ethnic groups cultivate hand in hand

Your dream flower will bloom every inch of the land of China

第一篇章

国之大

心之厦

筑梦华夏

每个中国人
心中都印有骄傲的图腾
那是中华大地不息的血脉传承
那是华夏儿女共有的壮美之梦
这梦的回音
响彻在巍峨挺立的群山之巅
响彻在现代化的工厂车间
更响彻在你我的心田
这梦的模样
是阳光少年奋发的青春脸庞
是乡间山清水秀的焕然景象
是一艘艘巨轮远航的笛声悠长
是烈日下工人们辛勤的汗水流淌
这梦的画卷
将由十四亿双手齐力绘就打造
它还将被赋予脉搏和心跳

与这片土地和人民相拥舞蹈
它将见证伟业功成
亦将迎来世界的惊叹与聚焦
那将是神州之光的璀璨登场
带着五千年的痛饮咏叹
于寰宇间傲世闪耀

Build the Dream of China

Every Chinese

Has a proud totem in the heart

That is the continuous blood heritage of China

That is the magnificent dream cherished by Chinese people

The echo of the dream

Resounds on the top of lofty mountains

Resounds in the modern factory workshops

Even resounds in our hearts

The image of the dream

Is the young faces of vigorous teenagers

Is the beautiful scenery of the countryside

Is the long whistles of oceangoing vessels

Is the sweat of workers in the scorching sun

The picture of the dream

Surely will be built by billion pairs of hands together

It also will be given pulse and heartbeat

It will hug and dance with the land and people

It will see the great achievements

Also will get the world's exclamation and focus

That will be the resplendent appearance of the light of China

With the swig and chant for five thousand years

Shining proudly in the universe

第一篇章　国之大　心之厦

是你

——敬献给伟大光荣的中国共产党

是你
用苍劲的臂膀
托起火红的朝阳
把威武的雄鸡
照得金亮

是你
用钢铁的脊梁
托起华夏的希望
让辽阔的神州
处处花香

是你
用坚定的目光
聚焦伟大的梦想
让泱泱中华
迎风远航

我们坚信

在这片土地上

永远都会有一种力量

一种信仰

领着我们

向前方

第一篇章 国之大 心之厦

It's You

——Dedicated to the Great and Glorious
Communist Party of China

It's you

With strong arms

Raise up the flaming red sun

The mighty rooster

Is shined bright gold

It's you

With steel backbone

Raise up the hope of Huaxia

Make the vast China

Filled with the fragrance of flowers everywhere

It's you

With a determined look

Focus on great dreams

Make our great China

Sail against the wind

We do believe

On this broad land

There is always a power

A kind of faith

Leading us

To march forward

第一篇章　国之大　心之厦

伫立在历史画卷前

伴着黄河的怒吼浩荡

映着喜马拉雅的圣洁雪光

浸润着纯净无瑕的茉莉馨香

历史画卷如光影铺陈过往

凝结智慧的四大发明彰显着华夏非凡

丝绸之路的驼铃声依然回响耳畔

逐鹿中原的铁马硝烟仿佛仍在眼前

大唐盛美的霓裳正歌舞蹁跹

无情的战火和侵略者的狰狞印刻出血泪苦难

我看到无数仁人志士舍身卫国力保家园

他们用顽强与信仰终迎来曙光重现

为这片土地撑起一片安宁的天

后人没有理由不万般珍惜 接续向前

百业待兴 斗志无限

如今的神州大地

生机焕发 春色无边

山河底色缤纷明艳

画卷与时光相拥延展

它定将呈现壮阔瑰丽的奇景佳篇

Standing in Front of Historical Scroll

As the mighty Yellow River growls

Reflecting the light of holy Himalayan snow

Immersing in the fragrance of pure jasmine flowers

The past is shown in the historical scroll

Four Great Inventions highlight China's extraordinary genius

Camel bells of the Silk Road still echo in my ears

The brutality of throne-seizing fights appears

The gorgeous feather garment of Tang Dynasty is singing and dancing

Merciless wars and ferocious invaders incur miserable tears

I see countless noble martyrs defend our homeland without fears

By their tenacity and faith the dawn at last reappears

They hold up a peaceful sky for this land and our well-being

The following generations should spontaneously cherish and keep going

We will prosper all trades as our morale is rising

The Divine Land today

Abounds with vibrant vigor and splendid scenery of spring

The background of the mountains and rivers is so colorful and bright

The scroll and time are embracing and extending

On it a magnificent future will assuredly be happening

第一篇章

国之大 心之厦

千载雄关诉峥嵘

如果能够穿越时光隧道

我想竹杖芒鞋轻快如飞鸟

去感受千载雄关烽火的温度

去抚摸硝烟尚未散尽的垛口

那绵延千里的沉默砖瓦

曾阻挡多少入侵的敌族

那肃穆的工事巨阵

翻越崇岭巍峨

跨过干涸大漠

无悔奔向天高海阔

这纵横七省的古道雄关

令世人惊鸿喟叹

它见证着悠悠千载

诉说着峥嵘澎湃

所有的恩怨争斗

被黄沙掩埋

与斑驳同在

这屹立千年的万里雄关

已然化作这片土地的灵魂铠甲

精神盾牌

The Great Wall Narrates
Thousands of Extraordinary Years

If I could go through the time tunnel

I would want to be unconstrained like a swift bird

To feel the temperature of beacon fire on the grand pass dating

back thousands of years

To touch the crenels with the residual smoke of gunpowder

Those silent bricks and tiles stretching thousands of miles

Ever prevented many invading enemies

The solemn and giant fortifications

Pass over the lofty mountains

Cross the dry desert

Rush to the high sky and wide sea resolutely

The ancient grand pass crossing seven provinces

Is amazing the whole world

It bears witness to the history of thousand years

It tells the fierceness of the extraordinary years

All of the grievances and fights

第一篇章

国之大 心之厦

Have been covered by yellow sand

Staying with the mottle

The grand pass standing for thousands of years

Has become the soul armor

And the spirit shield of this land

大山深处的笑颜

高耸险峻的群山
挡住了一双双好奇清澈的眼
更切断了通往繁华的连线
茫茫的戈壁荒滩
拒绝了绿意萌发的虔诚心愿
只留给天空一方枯黄的脸
辛勤劳作年复一年
那破旧的屋檐
依然是眼中最高的天
乡亲的愁苦与期盼
在新时代迎来了地覆天翻
选派干部扎根深山
科技能手技术支援
文化帮扶启智发展
更有山海对口携手并肩
苦了几代的老乡
看到了黑山变绿
住进了明亮新居
自家的瓜果畅销千里

家园一派焕然生机

古稀老人如孩童般欢喜

老乡大叔不再紧锁眉心

他品尝到了新生活的舒心甜蜜

年轻人争相勤学技艺

工厂田间大比拼

随风摇曳的麦浪与潺潺小溪

正诉说着大山深处关于希望的奇迹

那一张张淳朴开怀的笑颜

就是幸福的谜底

Smiling Faces from Remote Mountains

Those steeply elevated mountains

Covered the pure and curious eyes

Even cut off the access to prosperity

The vast Gobi and desolate sand

Rejected the heartfelt wish for sprouting new green

Just left a dry and yellow face to the sky

These natives worked hard year after year

The dilapidated eaves

Were still the highest sky in their eyes

The folks' sorrow and expectation

Changed upside down in the new era

Designated cadres dedicate themselves to those mountains

Technology experts support with advanced skills

Culture helps to inspire intelligence development

Also the Coast—mountain Cooperation speeds economy further

Dear folks living in hardship for several generations

See the black mountains turn green

They move into bright new houses

Their fruits sell well to far away

The homeland is full of vitality

The old men feel so happy like lovely children

Uncle folk does not frown any more

He tastes the sweet honey of new life

Young men learn the new skills actively

Competitions take place in the factories and fields

The swaying wheat and the murmuring stream

Are telling the miracle of hope in the remote mountains

The simple and pleasant smiling faces

Are the answer to the riddle about happiness

驰骋苍茫

当记忆定格在远行的时刻
思绪便飞上了拥挤的火车
旅途被沉默的铁轨拉长交错
焦急的双眼与汽笛争相诉说
那漫长的摇晃啊
疲惫的睫毛长出厚厚的青苔
这一幕被嵌入相框慢慢泛黄
眼前是飞驰呼啸的钢铁游龙
是瞬间绝尘的闪电惊鸿
这犹如精灵般的现代交通
以攻坚为动力
以创新为引擎
成为广袤疆土上驰骋的奇迹
将苍茫大地舞动为一首豪迈的诗

Speeding Across the Vastness

When the memories freeze on the travel time

The thoughts fly to the crowded train

The trip is stretched by silent rails

The anxious eyes and whistle scramble to tell

The shaking journey is so long

That the thick moss grows from eyelashes

This scene has been kept in photo frame and turned yellow

Now we see the steel dragon speeding and whistling

It's the lighting glimpse

The modern fairy transportation

Overcoming difficulties is the impetus

Creation is the engine

This has become the miracle speeding across the vastness

It turns into a heroic poem written on the great land

毅心抗疫

己末庚初
乌云将晴朗猝然驱逐
一方薄薄的口罩
阻挡了渴盼已久的回家路
一双双忧愁的眼睛
写满惶恐与无助
我听到来自远方的啼哭
就在此刻
一个声音划破长空
一个个坚毅无畏的身影
勇赴荆楚战场
来不及再望一眼深情的双眸
来不及再亲一下可爱的小手
来不及再听一声那慈祥的温柔
因为他们已化身勇士
必须冲在前头
记不清多少个黑夜与白昼
他们持续作战一丝不苟
当看到病患好转康复

他们才会露出会心笑容
从不顾自己是否面容全非或是满身伤痛
毅力是他们的坚固盾牌
热爱使他们初心不改
这场没有硝烟的战争
终会以我们的胜利而成为历史的峥嵘对白

Perseverance Fighting Against Epidemic

At the end of Year of Ji Hai

The black clouds drived the sun away suddenly

A thin square mask

Blocked the way home

The worried eyes

Full of fear and helplessness

I hear the crying from far away

At this moment

A voice is piercing the sky

Firm and fearless figures

Go bravely to the battlefield in Hubei

No time to look at the affectionate eyes

No time to kiss the lovely little hands

No time to hear the kind tenderness

Because they have become warriors

They must rush to the front

Many days and nights

They fight consistently and conscientiously

第一篇章

国之大 心之厦

028

When they see the patient get recovery

They will smile happily

Regardless of their own hurts or pains

Perseverance is their solid shield

They never change their original aspiration because of love

This battle without smoke

Will become a unique historic dialogue for our victory

情迷飞天

心中的，梦里的，前世今生的

都在这一刻陶醉融化

我来到了神奇的敦煌

我走进了谜一样的莫高

四周巧夺天工的精彩壁画

让眼睛应接不暇

一幅幅美轮美奂的千年经典

让心开出怒放的花

你那柔曼的衣襟

让历史如浮云般清逸飘洒

你那多彩的裙裾

激起片片柔情

随着历史的尘埃化作天边火红晚霞

你轻拨琴弦，反弹琵琶

让历史响起仙乐飘飘

柳眉，凤眼，樱唇

勾勒出历史的妩媚与多情

更让欣赏者领略人类的伟大神话

你那飘飞的舞姿
触动着人们翱翔的梦想
让心在彩云深处
寻觅到共同栖息的家
那一尊尊雄伟雕塑
历经千年依然神采奕奕
这是佛的不老金身
更是历史艺术的璀璨奇葩

我徜徉在这辉煌瑰丽的艺术宫殿
我迷失在这奇幻无比的灵魂乐园
感悟着历史的沧桑
惊叹着先人的力量
多想穿越时光的隧道
去领略昔日的繁华
多想拥有飞天的双翅
去亲吻那一朵朵洁白的童话

深情地凝望着这绝世的美丽

心中升腾起无限遐想

这生于西北的瑰宝

是华夏文明之树开出的绚丽之花

那倾世的容颜

将永远装点着历史青翠的枝桠

Intoxicated with Flying Apsaras

In my heart, in my dreams, and across the long past life

All of the things are being enchanted and melted

I come to the mysterious Dunhuang

I enter the enigmatic Mogao Grottoes

And see the magnificent frescoes around me

My eyes are enjoying a feast

Of thousand–year–old splendid classic

My heart is filled with flowers blooming fervently

Your soft and light veils

Let the history be as elegant as a floating cloud

Your colorful and beautiful skirt

Arouses pieces of tender feelings

That turns into a red sunset with the dust of history

You pluck the strings of Pipa behind your back

Making history ringing with fairy music

Willow cycbrow, phoenix eye, cherry lip

Outline the charm and passions of history

And let the viewer appreciate the great myth of mankind

Your flying dance

Touches everyone's dream of flying

Let the hearts in the depth of the clouds

Find the common inhabited dwelling

The magnificent statues

Still fresh after a thousand years

This is the Buddha's golden body

It's also a splendid flower of history and art

I wander in this magnificent palace of art

I'm lost in this fantastic paradise of soul

Feeling the vicissitudes of history

Marveling at the power of ancestors

How I want to go through the tunnel of time

To appreciate the past prosperity

How I wish I had wings

To kiss the white fairy tales

Gazing affectionately at the unique beauty

My heart is filled with infinite reverie

The treasure born in the northwest

Is the splendid flower of the tree of Chinese civilization

The face amazing the world

Will forever adorns the verdant branches of history

第一篇章

国之大

心之厦

一叶沸海

世间草木万千

独获众心青睐者无多

唯有神奇叶片

穿越千年依然魅力不减

它长于山岭腰间

或排列为如画的梯田

适时采摘

历经繁复工艺

忍受高温与揉制

远比生活打压更为剧烈

当它入杯之时

迎来滚烫如刑的怀抱

它却如获重生

蹁跹舒展

如梦般浮沉飞旋

瞬间沸腾了一片海

幻化交融

遂见色之澄澈香之沁脾

轻抿入喉

暖透心海

复品数杯

往事悠然于怀

经年饮之

静彻淡泊神思辽阔

油然而生对大自然的感恩热爱

及世事之平和谦态

我惊诧于这草木的叶片

竟能同时造就醇厚与清冽

这分明是人间清泉

饮之恒恋

One Leaf Boils the Whole Sea

Thousands of grasses and trees in the world

There is very few being the public favorites

Only the magic leaf

Has great charm lasting for thousand years

It grows on the hillsides

Or lines into beautiful terrace fields

Picked at the right time

It goes through many processes

That mostly high temperature and twisting

Is much severer than the blows of life

When it's put into the cup

It embraces torture–like heat

However it thus gains rebirth

Spreading and turning around

Whirling up and down like dreams

Boiling the whole sea for an instant

Changing and melting

Then the clear color and refreshing fragrance appear

Take a sip gently

The heart is completely warm

Drink a little more

All the past is in the mind leisurely

Drink it for years

We will enjoy inner serenity and broad thinking

Will be grateful to the nature

Also be peaceful and modest

I am so astonished by the leaf

It does create mellow and crystal–clear tastes in the same time

This is really the clear spring in the world

Eternal love for drinking

第
一
篇
章

国
之
大

心
之
厦

涅槃凝彩

跳动的火焰

炼制着昼夜蔓延

绕指柔的可爱泥盏

羽化弥坚

水墨丹青的妙笔

经历酷刑考验

升华为永固凝彩

这是源于东方的奇慧匠心

成就涅槃重生的工艺臻品

山岭之土何以惊艳蜕变

因它经受住残酷的熬煎

因它起身于平实的地面

那妙手绘就的图案

历经岁月变幻依然鲜活饱满

那悦目的色彩

不惧尘封与遗忘

永葆初颜

惊艳了时光的脸

Color Condensed in Nirvana

Dancing fire

Refining all day and all night

The lovely gentle clay cups

Begin to turn strong and tough

The masterstroke of ink and wash

Going through the torture test

Sublimating to color condensed

This is outstanding wisdom and originality of the Orient

Making exquisite craftsmanship after nirvana and rebirth

Why does the mountain soil metamorphose amazingly

Because it has withstood cruel suffering

Because it roots in plain ground

The designs by skilled hands

Still fresh and bright

The attractive colors

Do not fear gathering dust and being forgotten

Forever keep the initial appearance

Amazing face of time

第一篇章

国之大 心之厦

千帆奋楫新时代

当一轮红日从海平面喷薄而出
我听到浪潮浩荡的巨大声响
这是新时代的磅礴力量
这是梦想征程的振奋号角
它鼓舞着每一位弄潮儿女
奋楫破浪勇拼敢闯
在这条梦想的航道上
万千儿女以破浪前行为乐
以奋进争先为荣
这艘梦想的巨轮
将在众心砥砺中巍然进发
终抵粲然彼岸

Thousand Ships Struggle to Paddle in the New Era

When the red sun gushes out from the sea level

I hear tremendous sound of the vast waves

This is the tremendous power of new era

This is the inspiring clarion call of dream journey

It encourages every wave rider

To break waves and fight bravely

On this dream channel

Thousands of marines take pleasure in breaking waves

They are proud of striving to be the first

These giant ships of dream

Will sail forward majestically by uniting as one

To reach the bright destination

第一篇章

国之大 心之厦

第二篇章

乡之遥
情之切

Chapter Two

Sincere Feelings for
Faraway Hometown

乡童恋忆

遥远的山村
青青的竹林
藏着儿时的纯真
蜿蜒的小溪
流淌童年的记忆
水底顽皮的石头
浸湿梦的衣襟
灵巧的镰刀
舞动疯长的岁月
可爱的背篓
装满外公的叮咛
一方矮墙
挡住最初的慌张
梦里的故乡
让漂泊的心靠航
那棵屋后的小树
一定开满了鲜花
嫩绿满枝桠

Memories and Love of Countryside Childhood

In the mountain village far away

Green bamboo forests

Hides the innocence of childhood

The winding stream

Flowing the memory of my childhood

The naughty stones under the water

Wet the lapel of my dreams

The smart sickle

Dances on the swift years

The lovely basket—on—back

Is full of grandpa's warm exhortation

A low wall

Blocks the original panic

The hometown in my dreams

Lets the wandering heart rely

The little tree behind the old house

Must be in bloom

The branches merge in tender green

第二篇章

乡之遥 情之切

一声乡音　萦耳驻心

成长的时光有着漂泊的气质

脚步丈量几多寒冷与烈日

背包里装着故乡与倔强心事

路过摩天森林

我看见天空严肃的倒影

耳边是都市的交响和鸣

路过繁花满墙的街巷

我看见人间烟火暖意洋洋

耳边突然传来熟悉的乡音

好似珍宝忽从心底翻出声响

瞬间将我带回那片竹海茫茫

欣喜邂逅

这一声异乡的奖赏

踏着音符轻盈歌唱

我看见那弯新月正在树梢梳妆

A Local Accent Echoes in My Ears and Mind

Growing time is full of wandering temperament

The footsteps measure cold and hot days

Hometown and stubborn mind are put in backpack

Walking past skyscrapers

I see the serious reflection of sky

I hear the symphony of the city

Passing by the streets with flowers blooming all over the walls

I see the warmth of earthly joys

Hearing the familiar accent by chance

Just like taking the treasures out of heart suddenly

I am taken back to the bamboo grove for an instant

Meeting unexpectedly and happily

This prize of foreign land for me

Light singing with musical note

I see the crescent moon is making herself up

第二篇章

乡之遥 情之切

麻辣欢味

蜀于西南隅

竹海无垠翠立

川字何其简约

三个辣椒调皮排列

勾勒出巴蜀儿女火一般的热情不灭

恰如那挚爱的麻辣

是永不更改的滚烫牵挂

无论清寒冬腊

抑或酷暑炎夏

始终渴盼那舌尖上的乡味之花

无论身处何地

愈远离愈寻觅

麻味唤香

同引辣痛淋漓

离乡千里万里

饱满畅悦瞬间直抵

Happy Taste of Spice and Pepper

Situated in the Southwest of China

Sichuan boasts vast bamboo forest

Its abbreviation name is so simple

Like three hot peppers line up naughtily

Describing the Sichuaneses' great enthusiasm

Just like the favorite spice and pepper

Is the never changing deep concerning

Whether it is cold winter

Or hot summer

I always yearn for the hometown delicacy

Wherever I live

The further I go, the more I desire it

The numbing taste arouses the flavor of the dish

And I enjoy the spicy flavor heartily at the same time

Thousands of miles away from hometown

The pleasant taste brings me back instantly

第二篇章

乡之遥 情之切

心海竹林

家乡的竹林

是可爱村落最独特的景致

常年拥着悦目的翠绿

守护着袅袅炊烟与乡村欢颜

家乡的竹林

是儿时亲近的伙伴

它聆听过多少天真的欢笑

收藏了多少孩提的心事

竹林中儿时的欢笑

是记忆中最动听的风铃

随着季节的飘荡

时时发出悦耳的声响

这美妙的声音

伴我度过勤苦艰辛的年少时光

也伴我走过所有闪光与黯淡

竹林婆娑的倩影

是镌刻于心醉人的芳踪

竹林的美

带着远离尘嚣的宁静

也带着抛却世俗的清新

我常想

真正端庄优雅的女子

应该也拥有如竹林般卓绝的风姿

竹林的姿态

是成长路上永恒的标杆

每当遭遇困苦磨难

竹林的英姿浮现脑际

给我无声的鞭策与鼓励

如有一种物象

诠释思乡情结

我想那一定是竹林

这一抹青翠的绿

已在生命中化为一片海

陪伴我坚定远航

初心不改

Bamboo Forest in the Sea
of My Heart

The bamboo forest of my hometown

Is the most unique scenery of the lovely village

It shows beautiful emerald green all the year round

While guarding the serene life and happiness of the village

The bamboo forest of my hometown

Was a close fellow of my childhood

It heard a lot of innocent laughter

And kept many secrets of a child's heart

The happy laughter in the bamboo forest

Is the most beautiful jingle in my memory

Floating with seasons

Making a pleasant sound

The wonderful sound

Accompanied me through the youth of diligence and hardship

And all the happiness and sadness

The beautiful figure of the swaying bamboo forest

Is the beautiful trace in my heart

The beauty of bamboo forest

Contains the peace far from bustle

And the unworldly freshness

I often think

That a truly elegant lady

Should have extraordinary temperament same as bamboo forest

The upright posture of bamboos

Is the eternal benchmark on the way of growth

When I meet with difficulties

A straight bamboo arises in my mind

Encouraging me silently

If there is an image

Can represent hometown sentiment

I surely believe that is bamboo forest

The splash of emerald green

Has turned into a sea in my life

Accompanies me to sail forward firmly

Original aspiration never changes

第二篇章

乡之遥

情之切

忆之芽

西南一隅

无名山崖

斜生出一株倔强的芽

于缝隙中破土

在绝望里开花

仰望飞鸟的天堂

俯瞰鱼虾戏浪

安然享受阳光的慈祥

默默承受寒冬刺骨的伤

流言蜚语

那是风在说着情话

风雨雷电

是天空在调皮玩耍

四季流转

始终在枝头粲然

陪伴着孤单女孩

七载冬夏

携手成长

共同坚强

在霓虹灯闪烁的异乡

心底依然安放这颗记忆的芽

给她希望

给她力量

无悔前行

相拥怒放

Bud of Memory

In a corner of Southwest

The nameless cliff

Grows a stubborn bud obliquely

It breaks through the earth and gap

Blooms in despair

Looks up at the birds' heaven

Overlooks the fish playing in waves

Enjoys the kindness of sunshine

Silently bears the bitter cold of winter

All of the gossips

Are the love words by wind

Storm, thunder and lightning

Are the naught playing of sky

Seasons have been changing

It smiles on the branches all the time

Accompanying the lonely girl

For seven years of winter and summer

They grow hand in hand

And be strong together

Live in the foreign land with neon flashing

This bud of memory is still kept in her heart

Giving her hope

Giving her strength

She struggles forward without any regret

They bloom fully together

第二篇章　乡之遥　情之切

端详往昔

数载之后

我又回到了这里

回到了见证我峥嵘青春的小天地

那曾经给予我心灵养分的书籍

还有陪伴过我无数个夜晚的随身听

依然排列得十分整齐

还有那素雅的日记本

仿佛还依稀可见当年的泪滴

拂去封面的薄尘

那唯美的图案依然清晰

只是已褪去了当初的鲜活

仅剩沉静的表情

我不敢翻开那写满故事的昨日

怕自己会过于伤感而陷入海底

闭上双眼深深地呼吸

心中仍然渴望面对那段铅一般沉重的日子

每个字都是曾经的自己
每一笔都如针尖般细密
刺痛我的眼睛
透过晶莹细数昨日的点滴
好似在观赏一部励志的青春剧
那个女孩就这样长大
她走过了多少荆棘
为何在她脸上看不到愁苦
只有温暖和希冀
我好想抱着她哭
用我温柔的双臂
给她最深的怜爱与疼惜
好想看看她当初柔弱的身躯
是如何穿过冰冷的风雨
是否也曾经独自哭泣
我好想为她拭去泪滴
给她最真诚的慰藉与鼓励
或许我应该庆幸
女孩依然有着纯真的眸子

我不由惊叹时光的神奇
竟有如此化茧成蝶的魔力
它见证着所有努力
更考验着每个人的恒心
它将青丝染上霜雪
在光洁的额头刻下印记
它为不同的眼睛选映不同的风景
也为不同的灵魂搭配各色的外衣

不要嘲笑勤勉的人衣衫褴褛
或许只是一时拮据
有一天华丽转身
会让世人为之惊艳痴迷
更不要轻视任何一个小小的梦想
历经磨难与孤寂
待宝剑铸成
定有万丈光芒卓然耀世

有这样的信念支撑

就不惧怕曲折泥泞

只要坚定地跋涉

越过险滩与崎岖

隐忍坚持

永不放弃

就会看见辽阔平原与风光旖旎

这

就是时光的赠予

在苦涩中坚守奋争

终会品尝沁润心房的香醇甜蜜

Meditation and Memories
of the Past

After several years

I come back again

Back to the little world seeing my extraordinary youth

The books that once gave me spiritual nourishment

And the Walkman that has accompanied me for countless nights

Still in perfect order

In my simple but elegant diary–book

The tears of those years are still vaguely seen

Dust away from the cover

The artistic pattern is still clear

But the freshness and aliveness have disappeared

Just the calm expression is left

I dare not open the stories which record yesterday

Afraid of being too sentimental and drowning in the sea

I close my eyes and breathe deeply

Still eager to face the heavy days

Every word is my previous self

Every stroke is as meticulous as a needle

Stings my eyes

Count every detail of yesterday through crystal tears

Just like watching an inspirational Youth Drama

So the girl grows up

How many thorns she has gone through

Why can't you see sorrow on her face

You can only see warmth and hope

I really want to cry while hugging her

With my gentle arms

Give her the deepest love and affection

I do want to see how her weak body

Got through the cold wind and rain

Has she ever cried alone

I really want to wipe away her tears

Give her the most sincere comfort and encouragement

Maybe I should rejoice

For the girl still has pure and innocent eyes

I can't help marveling at the magic of time

That transforms a cocoon into a butterfly

It witnesses all of the efforts

第
二
篇
章

乡
之
遥

情
之
切

Even tests everyone's perseverance

It dyes the black hair with white frost and snow

Ploughs the mark on the smooth forehead

It shows different views for different eyes

Also for different souls with different colors of coat

Don't laugh at the diligent men for their shabby clothes

Maybe it's just a temporary constraint

Someday a magnificent turn

Will make the world amazed and fascinated

Don't despise any little dream

Through hardships and loneliness

When the sword is cast

There must be a brilliant light shining on the world

Supported by this firm belief

We will not be afraid of arduous journeys

Just walk firmly

Crossing dangerous shoals and rough terrain

With patience and persistence

Never give up

Then we will see the vast plains and exquisite scenery

This

Is the gift of time

Persevering in bitterness

Finally will taste the mellow sweetness moisturizing the heart

鹭岛之春满秋韵

曾经多少年

任凭光阴滑过指尖

曾经多少次

想要记住岁月的脸

记忆的河

带着珍珠与沙砾

无悔地奔涌向前

终于

在这个春天

我邂逅了最美的诗篇

那带着悲壮与重生的飞旋

演绎出天地间最深沉的爱恋

我深知这凄美的舞动

不仅是惊艳的瞬间

更是一种伟大的成全

在盎然满园的鹭岛春天

正上演着一场金色的绝恋

春风温润

满眼蹁跹

一时恍惚

这分明是丰盈之秋

却为何新绿绵延

难道春也是落叶的眷恋

抑或是秋天还未散场的盛宴

这漫天飞舞的金蝶

幻化为时光的仙子

呈现给人们有着浓浓秋韵的别致春天

这是时光的错位

还是鹭岛的神奇

或许并非所有问题都需要答案

如果是恩赐

就请停止一切追问

静心享受这梦幻般的绚烂

一如生命中曾出现的那些惊喜片断

我们欣然珍藏

不带一丝疑虑杂念

我伫立在春叶飞舞的季节之畔

感受这来自时光与自然的极致浪漫

闭上双眼

我仿佛听见岁月的脚步

轻盈而果敢

不再如往昔般孤独蹒跚

Xiamen Island's Spring has the Charm of Autumn

So many years

The time has elapsed without lingering

So many times

I want to remember the face of years

The river of memories

That brings pearls and sands

It running forward without regrets

Finally

In this spring

There appears the most beautiful poem I've ever met

The swirl with rebirth and heroic tragedy

That's the deepest love in the world

I deeply know the poignant dance

Is not only the amazing moment

Furthermore, it is the great fulfillment

In the flourishing spring of Xiamen Island

There is a golden love

With the warm spring breeze

第二篇章

乡之遥
情之切

Everything is dancing

I fall into a dreamy world faintly

This is clearly the height of autumn

But why does so much green stretch

Is spring also the attachment of fallen leaves

Or is it a feast that has not yet dispersed of autumn

The golden butterflies are flying all over the sky

They turn into the fairies of time

Presenting a distinctive spring with the charm of autumn features

Is this aberration of changing seasons

Or is it the magic of Xiamen Island

Maybe not all questions need answers

If it's a gift

Please stop asking

Just enjoy the dreamy glamour quietly

Same like those surprise memories in life

We keep them in mind pleasantly

Without any doubt and distracting thought

I'm standing in the season with spring leaves flying

Feeling the ultimate romance from time and nature

Closing my eyes

I seem to hear the pace of time

Light and gutsy

No longer lonely and tottering as past

天堂海

蓝色的海洋

轻波微漾

好似青春的涟漪激荡

温柔海草

静静凝望

身边的鱼儿快乐徜徉

大海就是幸福的天堂

那里没有冰封的心墙

只有纯洁目光

将一切荡涤得清澈明亮

我漫步海边

陶醉在海天一色的纯美景象

海风咸涩

吹起忧伤

晶莹的惆怅溢满眼眶

我的天堂

是否在那深深海底

童话的故乡

Heaven Sea

The blue sea

Light waves are slightly rippling

As if the youth surging

The gentle seaweeds

Are gazing quietly

The fishes around are swimming happily

Sea is the heaven of happiness

There is no frozen wall in heart

It only has the pure eyes

That clean up everything clear and bright

I walk by the sea

Intoxicated by the purely beautiful scene of sky melting in the sea

Sea wind is salty and bitter

Blowing my sorrow

The glistening melancholy captures my eyes

The heaven of my own

Is it under the sea

The hometown of fairy tales

第三篇章

校之纯美
梦之可期

Chapter Three

The Beauty of School is Pure,
the Dream is Worth Expecting

芳菲·集美

浔江畔

灵秀一隅

恢宏壮丽

镌刻心底

书声朗朗

汇成动人交响

青春身影

牵动无数深情目光

梦想在这里启航

乘风破浪

到达心中的远方

白鹭翱翔的双翅

拍动少年一飞冲天的豪情

灼灼智慧

闪耀永恒的诚毅之光

这里是共同的心灵家园

回荡着青涩的记忆

铭刻着青春的理想

幽幽小径

让年少的心事曲折神秘

红硕木棉

让青春的情怀绚丽飞扬

梦想是青春的宿命

所有纯美只为年轻的心浓情绽放

那一夜

遥望星空

最亮的一颗

是你我引以为荣的

嘉庚星

Luxuriant · Jimei

The bank of Xunjiang

A delicately pretty corner

Extensively magnificent

Engraves on the bottom of my heart

The reading sound is loud and clear

Converges into a moving symphony

The youth figures

Grip countless affectionate eyes

Dreams are sailing forth from here

Through winds and waves

Reaching the aspired distance

The flying wings of egrets

Encourages youth's soaring pride

Bright wisdom

Is shining eternal light of sincerity and perseverance

Here is the common spiritual home

Echoing the green memories

With the ideal of youth engraved

The quiet path

Lets young minds be tortuous and mysterious

The red large kapok flowers

Inspire the feelings of youth to fly

Dream is the destiny of youth

All pure beauty blooms only for the young hearts

That night

Looking at the sky

The brightest star in the sky

That makes you and me proud

Is called Tan Kah Kee Star

第三篇章 校之纯美 梦之可期

园丁情怀

心中的舞台

在一双双清澈的眼眸前展开

所有的喜悦澎湃

都挥洒于心爱的讲台

父辈的疼爱

朋友的关怀

在这里

从未更改

清脆的铃声

是最动听的告白

一串串精彩

一场场豪迈

汇成人生激情似海

你执着守望

那片稚嫩的桃李

是否会如期迎来醉人华彩

等待

让如花的承诺

在风中绽开

Gardener's Feelings

The stage in my heart

Spreads out before pairs of limpid eyes

All of the joy and surge

Devote to the beloved platform

Love of elders

Care of friends

Are always here

And never change

The clear bell

Is the most attractive confession

A string of wonderful times

And the deep feelings of heroic

Converge into a sea of passion

You single-mindedly cultivate

Those young and vigorous students

Will they meet an intoxicating future as expected

Keep waiting

The promise like a flower

Will bloom in the wind

第三篇章　校之纯美　梦之可期

舞之恋

穿越凌霄

每一片云都是彩虹的牵挂

风儿阵阵

送来温柔衣裳

伴着星光起舞

脚步孤独

旋律是心中甜蜜的音符

夜幕下的舞者

为梦而跃动

那精灵般的飞旋啊

化作琴弦

奏出动人爱恋

飘向遥远

Affection of Dance

Crossing the sky

Every flake of cloud is the concern of rainbow

The wind blows

Bringing the soft clothes

Dancing with the starlight

The footstep is lonely

The melody is the sweet note

The dancer in the night

Leaps for the dreams

The rotating is like a fairy

It turns into strings

Plays moving melody of love

That flies afar

希望之旅

飞奔旷野

双腿永无止境地延伸

汗水是生命最好的点缀

把世界装进胸膛

伸开双臂

拍打金色的翅膀

让风为我加油

阳光给我万缕慈祥

侧耳听去

尽是青春的歌唱

多么高亢

犹如梦中的希望

告别疲惫

继续精彩的繁忙

Journey of Hope

Run in the wilderness

Legs extend endlessly

Sweat is the best decoration to life

Put the world in my chest

Open arms

Flapping the golden wings

Let the wind cheer for me

The sunshine gives me much kindness

Please listen

It's all the singing of youth

How resounding

Just like the hope in dream

Forget all the tiredness

Continue enjoying the busy spectacle

第三篇章

校之纯美　梦之可期

心湖

宁静湖心

映出无数青春身影

木桥曲折延伸

恰似故事离合的背景

串串脚印

揭开小说的结局

岸边繁茂的精灵

享受四季冷暖心情

新绿与枯萎

听从时节的命令

欣喜与落寞

告诉闪烁的繁星

它们会凝神倾听

永远忠诚守信

梦想似浮萍

随着风向漂移

吹散了随遇而安的蒲公英

留下勇敢的风信子

点缀湖畔的苍翠神秘

衬托木棉的妖娆淡定

绕湖而行

偶闻筑梦者轻柔低吟

惆怅写于眉心

不安归于平静

我的湖心

是谁投下顽皮的石

激起圈圈涟漪

扰乱鱼儿的清梦

骤然初醒

Heart Lake

The quiet center of lake

Reflects many figures of youth

The wooden bridge zigzag extends

Just like the background of joy and sorrow in the stories

Strings of footprints

Unveil the ending of novel

Luxuriant trees around the lake

Enjoy the warm and cold mood of the seasons

The fresh green and withering

Obey the order of seasons

Delight and loneliness

Tell the sparkling stars

They will listen attentively

They will be faithful and trustworthy forever

Dreams are same as the duckweeds

Drifting with the wind

That also blows away the aimless dandelion clocks

Leaving the brave hyacinths

Decorating the mysterious and verdant lakeside

Setting off the charm and calmness of kapok trees

Walking around the lake

I overhear the dream makers whispering softly

Melancholy is shown on their faces

Uneasiness returns to peace

In my heart lake

Who drops the naughty stones

Stirring up ripples

Disturbing the dreaming fish

That they wake up suddenly

第三篇章　校之纯美　梦之可期

恒咏学村

每当我漫步浔江之滨，
那阵阵潮音，
仿佛正掷地有声地讲述着一位老人的故事。

每当我遥望美丽学村，
那一幢幢嘉庚建筑，
仿佛正气宇轩昂地宣告着她骄傲的身世。

每当我驻足如画的校园，
那翩飞的白鹭，
仿佛正惬意欢畅地传递着家园的喜讯。

每当我仰望浩瀚星空，
那颗闪烁着独特光芒的星斗，
仿佛正殷切慈祥地注视着这片深情的土地。

这里，曾在荆棘中开辟光明的坦途，
这里，曾在危亡时托起未来的希望，
这里，曾在战火中书写壮美的青春，
这里，曾在苍白中书写奋进的华章！

这是一方承载着沧桑过往的厚重土地，

这是一方让异乡游子魂牵梦绕的挚爱家园，

这是一个令八方游客流连忘返的美丽学村，

这更是一座吸引无数学子深情向往的求学殿堂！

因为，她有一个独特的名字叫集美，

因为，她孕育了一位泽被后世的华侨领袖，

因为，她有值得后人传颂的永远闪光的故事，

因为，她拥有激励无数学子一生的伟大精神！

当你走进陈嘉庚纪念馆，

你会明白一个个美丽的故事原来都与这位老人有着不解之缘。

那一段段文字，

讲述着久远却仍然鲜活的故事。

那一帧帧相片，

让我们有幸瞻仰校主亲切的容颜。

校主的创举与伟业，我们无限感佩与自豪！

当你来到嘉庚故居，

你会明白一位南洋巨商缘何矢志报国且具如此感召力与影响力。

那一件件尘封的物品，

重现着校主艰苦勤勉的清廉之风。

那一幅幅题词，

见证着校主不仅是卓越的实业家，

更是华侨史与中国教育史一座不朽的丰碑！

当你看到校主与其胞弟共同订立的"诚毅"校训，
你会明白这看似简单的两个字有着多么丰富而深邃的内涵。
这最为简短的二字校训，
已成为万千集美学子一生践行的品行标杆，
更已成为海内外集美校友无比坚韧的精神纽带！

又是一季金黄时，
集美校园的木棉又飘起了飞絮，
凤凰木的枝头也已然告别花期，
唯有那相拥绽放的三角梅依然如夏般绚丽，
与一张张写满朝气的脸庞辉映着青春的美好。

此刻，我不禁合上书页闭目怀想，
这美如画卷的集美校园，定将上演更多的青春传奇。
因为，我们拥有共同的励志史，
因为，我们拥有共同的嘉庚印，
因为，我们拥有共同的诚毅魂！

Forever Ode to Jimei School Village

Every time I stroll along the coast of Xunjiang

The tidal waves

Seems to tell the story of an old man powerfully

Every time I look afar into the magnificent school village

The Tan Kah Kee Style Buildings

Seem to declare their proud life experience with an imposing

appearance

Every time I stand on the scenic campus

The flying egrets

Seem to deliver the good news from home happily

Every time I look up at the vast starry sky

The star twinkling with unique light

Seem to gaze at this loving land affectionately

It's here that a bright path opened up in thorns

It's here that an ardent hope held up in peril

第三篇章　校之纯美　梦之可期

It's here that a stirring youth recorded in war

It's here that a progressive chapter written in void

This is the land carrying years of suffering and hardships

This is the dear yearned homeland for wanderers

This is a magnificent school village attracting visitors from all directions

This is even more the palace of learning absorbing numerous students

Because she has a unique name Jimei

Because she gave birth to an overseas Chinese leader benefiting the later generations

Because she has the forever shining stories worthy of praise

Because she has the great spirit encouraging numerous students in their whole life

When you enter the Tan Kah Kee Memorial Museum

You will know all the beautiful stories have an indissoluble bond with this old man

The silent words

Are telling remote but still lively stories

The pictures there

Let us have the luck to see the kindly face of our school founder

We cherish admiration and pride for his great pioneering work and achievements

When you come to the Former Residence of Tan Kah Kee
You will understand why a Nanyang tycoon pledged to serve the
country with such charisma and influence
The dusty things there
Reproduce the diligent and upright style of the school founder
The inscriptions there
Prove that the school founder is not only an outstanding
industrialist
But an immortal monument in the history of overseas Chinese
and education in China

When you see the school motto "Sincerity and Perseverance"
set up by school founder and his brother
You will know the rich and profound connotation of these two
characters
The most concise school motto
Has become the moral standard for thousands of students of Jimei
Also has been a strong spiritual bond of Jimei alumni all over the
world

It's the golden season again
The kapok floats on Jimei campus
The royal poincianas have blossomed
Only the bougainvillea is still colorful as in summer
Reflecting the wonderful youth with the vigorous faces

第三篇章

校之纯美

梦之可期

At this moment, I close the book and think

The scenic Jimei campus will surely have more youth legends

Because, we have the common inspirational history

Because, we have the common mark of Tan Kah Kee

Because, we have the common soul of sincerity and perseverance

虹梦青春

青春若有梦

一定是彩虹的模样

高远纷呈

且有着奇异的芬芳

那一道用云汽凝结的桥

供弄潮儿奋勇踏浪

你问我

这般美好

为何只是一束短暂的光

我想告诉你

这是风雨之后最好的奖赏

Rainbow Dream of Youth

If youth has dreams

It must be like a rainbow

Lofty and colorful

With the special fragrance

The bridge is made of vapor

For the wave riders to conquer bravely

You ask me

So wonderful it is

Why is it just a momentary beam of light

I want to tell you

This is the best reward of a storm

世纪弦歌　初心永恒

——谨献给集美大学百年华诞

曾记否

1918 孟春时光

一位华侨实业家用情怀与信仰

在风雨中托起希望

举步维艰荆棘阻挡

依旧执着坚守从未彷徨

曾记否

闽海之滨的萧瑟黯淡

浔江之畔的盐碱荒滩

奇迹般地矗立起一片片精巧的红顶屋檐

那是校主的智慧独创

那是仅属于嘉庚建筑的壮美画卷

曾记否

校主亲自订立"诚毅"校训

铿锵二字 形简意广

蕴含着深情与期望

这是学校的灵魂

更是集大人永恒的基因与炽热血浆

曾记否

集美侨乡的校舍操场

最雅致的红砖楼房

还有那与白鹭相伴的书声朗朗

曾遭遇无情战火硝烟

颠沛流离几经创伤

曾记否

穿过数十载栉风沐雨的峥嵘沧桑

感恩领导亲切关怀

感恩贤达慷慨解囊

终圆校主宏愿

昔日渔村成为万千学子深深向往的求学殿堂

怎能忘

1994 季秋吉庆　百果飘香

五校合一　五指聚拳

集美大学挂牌组建

高等教育幸添纯美一隅

一片有着嘉庚印记与诚毅基因的梦想天堂

怎能忘

新校区恢宏气象

闽南风韵的燕尾脊诠释着民族风尚

明艳的嘉庚红洋溢着浓浓的古雅书香

如此钜美杰作

无愧百项经典工程之美誉嘉奖

怎能忘

2007 接受神圣检阅

教育部专家评估本科教学质量

全方位深度检测

优秀等级令人心潮激荡

更激起集大人百倍信心豪情万丈

怎能忘

校园生活精彩无限

莘莘学子越战越强

一次次激情演说 一次次唇枪舌战 一次次深情歌唱

享受挑战的快乐

也享受站在舞台上的自豪与荣光

怎能忘

一栋栋嘉庚楼宇古朴典雅

一条条林间小径清幽芬芳

还有那总是飘着佳肴香气的食堂

曾留下多少开怀时光与幼稚轻狂

都成为记忆深处永久的珍藏

永为傲

2003研究生教育零的突破

十载砥砺 挥汗无言

终迎来博士点庄严授权

集大人用踏实勤勉与坚韧顽强

不断续写骄人的历史华章

永为傲

全球最大"育德轮"教学实习船

是国家地方给力支持的最好体现

它承载着培育航海学子助力海上实践的使命担当

更承载校主为国力挽海权的宏大夙愿

它将镌刻着"诚毅"筑梦远方

永为傲

这片执着坚守与倾心耕耘的土地

终迎来硕果满枝 桃李芬芳

无论是胸怀全球劈波斩浪的弄潮儿郎

抑或杏坛争辉为国育才的杰出名师

都拥有同一个青春的故乡

永为傲

2008 九秩华诞

校主后裔与校友欢聚一堂

虽已分别多时

一声集大人 一声嘉庚弟子

总能让彼此无比亲切 热泪满眶

归来吧

2018 百年聚首共话情长

无论你身在八闽鹭岛还是异国他乡

母校真情的呼唤

校主深切的目光

都在等待你如约而至共享欢畅

归来吧

全球集大同窗

让我们在热情绚烂的凤凰树下重温昔日时光

一幕幕还是鲜活的模样

青春的梦想在这里学飞试航

这里是见证羽翼丰满的训练场

归来吧

踏进亲切的校园

见到一张张久违的脸庞

你将看到梦想分明正熠熠闪光

靠近彼此

青春的心仍然跳动在滚烫的胸膛

归来吧

穿越世纪的弦歌正响彻耳畔

初心澄澈 必将永驻心田

此刻 共同祝愿跨过世纪风雨的青春集大

在新时代波澜壮阔的伟大征程中

乘风破浪 巍然远航

Century String Songs
Eternal Initial Aspirations

——Dedicated to the Centenary of Jimei University

Do You Remember

In the early spring of 1918

An overseas Chinese industrialist with devotion and belief

Held up the hope in the hardships

Struggling hard and overcame the thorns

Still persisting without any hesitation

Do You Remember

The coast of Fujian was bleak and gloomy

The saline wasteland of the Xunjiang coast

Exquisite buildings with red root were erected magically

That was the wise creation by school founder

That only belongs to the magnificent scenery of Tan Kah Kee

building

Do You Remember

School founder set up the motto "sincerity and perseverance"

Two forceful characters Simple in form but broad in meaning

Containing deep feelings and expectations

This is the soul of school

Even more the eternal genes and hot blood of JMU people

Do You Remember

The school building and sports ground

The most elegant red brick buildings

And the sound of reading with the egrets

Once encountered the flames of war

Wandered with scarred wounds

Do You Remember

Through decades of suffering and hardships

Thanks the kind care of leaders

Thanks to the generosity of those worthy personages

The dream of school founder was finally realized

The old fishing village became the palace of learning expected

by thousands of students

We will never forget

The late autumn of 1994 with fruits fragrance

Five schools merged like five fingers of one fist

Jimei University was set up

Adding a corner of pure beauty to higher education

A dreamy paradise with the Tan Kah Kee mark and Chengyi gene

We will never forget

The magnificent sight of the new campus

The swallow tail ridge of South Fujian style shows the national fashion

Bright red of Tan Kah Kee style is full of traditional elegance

Such a great masterpiece

Worthy of 100 classic project awards

We will never forget

The significant review in the year of 2007

Experts from the Ministry of Education evaluated the quality of undergraduate teaching

With the comprehensive depth inspection

Everyone was excited for the excellent grade

It inspired JMU people's confidence and pride

We will never forget

The campus life is exceedingly wonderful

The students became increasingly in the competitions

Passionate speeches, battles of words, deep love singings

They enjoyed the happiness of challenge

And the pride and glory of standing on the stage

We will never forget

Tan Kah Kee buildings are simple and elegant

The paths in the woods are quiet and fragrant

And the dining hall that always has the smell of delicious food

Much happy and childish time were spent there

It's a permanent treasure in memory

Always be proud

The breakthrough in postgraduate education in the year of 2003

Ten years of hard work with sweat

Finally gained the solemn authorization of doctor's degree

We are diligent and indomitable

Continue to write proud historical chapters

Always be proud

The world's largest teaching practice ship "Yude"

Is the best embodiment of government strong support

It bears the mission of cultivating maritime students and helping

maritime practice

It also bears the school founder's grand aspiration of saving the sea power for our country

It struggles forward engraving "Sincerity and Perseverance"

Always be proud

This land is persevered and devoted to cultivation

The gained harvests are full of peaches and plums with fragrance

Whether it's a tide maker with a global mind

Or is it an outstanding teacher cultivating talents for the country

They all share the same hometown of youth

Always be proud

The ninetieth birthday in the year of 2008

The descendants of the school founder and alumni enjoyed a
happy gathering

Although separated for a long time

We are called JMUer, we are called Tan Kah Kee pupils

These names always make us intimate with tears

Come back home

Enjoy the centenary gathering and reveal the memories and love

Whether you are in Fujian or in a foreign country

The sincere call of your alma mater

The heartfelt look of our school founder

Are waiting for you to come as promised to share joys

Come back home

JMU schoolmates all over the world

Let's recall the past under the gorgeous flamboyant trees

All the memories are alive

The dream of youth was learning to fly here

Here is a training field for full wings

Come back home

Walk onto the familiar campus

seeing faces that haven't been seen for a long time

You will find the dreams still shining

Close to each other

The heart of youth is still beating in the enthusiastic chest

Come back home

The string song across the century is resounding clearly

The pure initial aspiration will be everlasting

At this moment, best wishes to our century−old yet youthful JMU

In the great journey of the new era

Ride the wind and the waves and sail forward majestically

第三篇章　校之纯美　梦之可期

第四篇章

峰之险峭
攀之以毅

Chapter Four

Climbing the Steep Peak with
Perseverance

守望坚强

伫立白桦林

血痕岁月如四季更替的心情

母亲的白发

亲手剪的窗花

一并藏进闪烁的繁华

华灯初上

行人匆忙

你可听见路边寂寥的歌唱

微笑与哭泣

都在遗忘哀伤

感受世界无常

更有永不改变的守望

望穿沧桑的海洋

岸边那伟岸的礁石

可是你不老的目光？

Keeping Strength

Standing in birch forest

Bloodstained years are like the mood of seasons

Mother's white hair

Window flowers made by myself

Hiding in the glittering prosperity

When the night begins

Pedestrians are in a hurry

Do you hear the lonely singing by the roadside

Smiling and crying

Are all forgetting sadness

Feel the changing world

And the forever expectation

Look through the vicissitudes of sea

The great rocks on the shore

Are your never aging eyes

第四篇章

峰之险峭 攀之以毅

逐梦天际

季节的风铃

在春风中轻吟低唱

于夏浪里欢快舞蹈

与秋叶一同飘零飞旋

向冬雪讲述纯洁爱恋

岁月的书签

阅尽时光流转

珍藏记忆片段

更有成长的阵痛

不忍丢弃一边

穿越尘世纷扰吧

向着最初的天空振翅翱翔

风雨打湿翅膀

沙尘阻挡航向

逆风的姿态永远是最美的模样

白云悠然

晴空蔚蓝

为梦想穿上柔曼衣衫

纵然黑夜来临

眼中依然闪烁明亮的星

期待黎明翩然而至

曙光粲然

照亮孤单的眼

奋飞的翼拨动生命琴弦

辽阔天际

待我书写华彩诗篇

Pursuing Dreams in the Sky

The wind chimes of seasons

Sing softly in the wind

Dance happily in the summer waves

Fly with autumn leaves

Talk about pure love to the snow

The bookmarks of years

Experience the elapsing time

Cherish the memories

The pain of growth

Will not be thrown away

Let's go through the earthly world

Flying towards the sky in heart

The wings get wet

Dust blocks the directions

Flying against the wind is the most beautiful attitude

Free white clouds

Clear blue sky

Dress the dream with gentle clothes

Even if the night comes

Bright stars still twinkle in the eyes

Looking forward to the dawn

The dawn is so bright

Lighting up the lonely eyes

Flying wings pluck the strings of life

The vast sky

Is waiting for me to write brilliant poems

第四篇章　峰之险峭　攀之以毅

心翼翱翔

儿时的梦想

长着缤纷的模样

穿越黑白岁月

依然熠熠闪光

历经漫长风霜

那双纤纤素手

是否还能拾起一片片晚秋的枯黄

时光的眼眸

无视季节的奔忙

它追随着太阳的脚步

傲视一切

从不犹豫彷徨

从不怜悯心伤

儿时的向往躲入尘封的行囊

带上温暖的微笑与孩子般新奇的眼光

向着湛蓝心空振翅翱翔

或许前方布满阴霾与苍凉

或许下一站就是失败与绝望

听着蜗牛的故事

眺望着远方的灯光

顿觉双翼充满力量

我不要浮华的琉璃与聒噪的喧嚣

只需一寸恬静的光阴

和一扇洒满阳光的窗

在每个伴着露珠的清晨

向着东方挥手问好

在漆黑静谧的深夜

梳理有些凌乱的羽毛

将世界安放于心空

为青春穿上素雅的衣裳

耳旁呼啸的风声

是双翼与天际的交响

Heart Wings Fly

The dreams of childhood

With colorful looks

Through the black and white years

Still shining

After many vicissitudes

That pair of slender hands

Can they still pick up the withered leaves of late autumn

Eyes of the time

Ignoring the season's bustle

They follow the sun

Distain everything

Never hesitate

Never pity or grieve

Childhood yearning hides in a dusty bag

With a warm smile and a childlike novelty

Flying towards the blue sky of heart

Perhaps the front is full of haze and desolation

Maybe the next stop is failure and despair

Listening to the story of snail

Overlooking the light in the distance

Suddenly the wings are full of strength

I don't want flashy glass or noisy hustle

I only need a little serene time

And a window full of sunshine

At every morning with dewdrops

Wave to the East and say hello

In the quiet dark night

Comb the messy feathers

Put the world in my heart

Wear the plain and elegant clothes for the youth

The whistling wind by the ear

Is a symphony of wings and sky

第
四
篇
章

峰
之
险
峭

攀
之
以
毅

勇者祭

陡峭山崖

孤独身影奋力攀爬

石缝中的绝望

开出妖冶的花

诀别一切诱惑迟疑

只带上微笑出发

所有质疑眼光

所有喧嚣嘈杂

被万道阳光淹没融化

耳旁呼啸的寒风

指尖嵌入的泥沙

绘成壮美的丹青妙画

或许一粒小小的石子

就能轻易粉碎这梦一般的神话

或许一次细微的偏差

就会输掉这场拼尽心力的厮杀

面对险峻

唯有进发

哪怕跌入无底深渊

也有高山为他祭奠牵挂

没有墓碑

没有鲜花

却有满目翠柏为他四季盎然如夏

这就是无畏者的代价

璨若烟火

亦如昙花

更似磐石

傲骨永铸

笑看繁华

Lament to the Brave

The steep cliff

The lonely figure is climbing hard

The despair in the crack of rock

Becomes charming flowers

Farewell to all temptation and hesitation

Setting up with smile

All of the doubts

All of the noise

Melted by the brilliant sunshine

The cold wind whistling by my ears

Dirt embedded on fingertips

Makes a magnificent picture

Maybe a little stone

Can easily crush the dreamy myth

Maybe a slight deviation

Will destroy this severe fight

Facing the tough peak

Going forward is the only path

Even if he falls into a bottomless abyss

The mountains will mourn for him

No tombstone

No flower

But there are ever-green cypresses stay exuberant

This is the price of the fearless

Bright as fireworks

Transient as epiphyllum

More like a rock

His pride lives forever

Calmly he watches the bustling world

第
四
篇
章

峰
之
险
峭

攀
之
以
毅

风景人生

二十三个年头
我看到人间无数的
悲欢离合
缘起缘落
我是命运的苦行僧
经历着太多的心酸与伤悲
有人大笑
为我的天真
有人叹息
为我的迟疑
我却藏在耳机里
听着自己心爱的歌曲
那些节奏
为人生而疯狂
那些歌者
为心情而流浪
我闭上眼睛
回到自己的家乡

Scenery of Life

In my twenty three years

I see countless

Grief at separation and joy in union of the world

Fate rises and falls

I am the ascetic monk of life

Experiencing too much sadness

Some people laugh

For my innocence

Some people sigh

For my hesitation

But I hide in my headphones

Enjoying my favorite songs

Those rhythms

Crazy for life

Those singers

Wandering for moods

I close my eyes

Going back to my hometown

载忆远航

窗外是阳光久违的慷慨

我看见跳舞的尘埃

犹如新绽的花儿忘情摇摆

我好奇地伸手去触摸

却被一阵疾风掩盖

惋惜着错过了跳动的精彩

独自在黄昏落寞徘徊

忆起孩童时竹林中的开怀

那般无邪

像是烦恼从未存在

长大是无法抵挡的悲哀

翅膀渐渐长出青苔

清澈的眼眸发育出无奈

奔跑的时光变得不再轻快

那棵老树告诉我

勇敢些 孩子

带上故乡

远方的世界才是属于你的未来

深深亲吻紫色的泥土

依然芬芳如梦中的花海

从未期待的离别

就此匆匆起航

途中惊涛骇浪

偶尔邂逅阳光

听从命运的舵

路过暗礁与恐慌

仍未见外面世界的模样

难道终点如桃花源般神秘无踪

抑或犹如海市蜃楼般虚无缥缈

一度失望心伤

渴望返航

回到竹林的怀抱

重温儿时的美好

梦想的双手将我带回

崎岖的轨道

纵然荆棘丛生

亦不能退缩避让

东方正值黎明

微微泛起光亮

那轮嫣红的朝阳

正温柔地向我问好

她正告别地平线

跃向永恒的东方

那喷薄的瞬间

将寰宇照亮

A Long Voyage with Memories

Outside the window is the long–lost sunshine

I see the dancing dust

Like a newly blooming flower swings freely

I try to touch it curiously

But it is blown by a gust

Regret missing the dancing brilliance

Wandering lonely at the twilight

I remember the childhood happiness in the bamboo forest

It's so innocent

Like trouble never existed

Growing up is inevitable sorrow

Moss grows on the wings gradually

Helplessness develops in the pure eyes

The running time is no longer brisk

The old tree tells me

Be brave my child

Remember hometown

The outside world belongs to your future

Kiss deeply the purple earth

第四篇章　峰之险峭　攀之以毅

130

Still fragrant like the flower fields in my dream

Never expected departure

I set sail in a hurry

Against the tempestuous waves on the way

I occasionally enjoy sunshine

Follow the rudder of fate

Pass by the reef and panic

I have still not seen the outside world

Is the destination so mysterious like Peach Blossom Spring

Or is it so illusory like the mirage

Once disappointed and upset

I was eager for returning

Rushing back to the bamboo forest

Reliving childhood happiness

Yet the hands of dream bring me

Back to the rugged road

Even so many thorns

Can't make me give up

It's dawn in the East

Slightly brighten up

The bright red sun

Is greeting to me gently

She's leaving the horizon

Leaping up to the eternal east

The moment of spurting out

Lights up the whole world

行者心囊

浓浓的迷雾

折射七彩阳光

有些刺眼

刺痛温柔的心房

身边的河流低语

与我对唱

唱出希望与理想

鱼儿快乐依然

不懂行人的凄凉

吐出一串串水泡

好似我的梦想啊

只是流星的辉煌

执着的脚步

奔向心中的归宿

义无返顾

哪怕太多的束缚

The Words of Mind on Life Journey

The thick fog

Refracts colorful sunshine

That dazzles my eyes

And stings my gentle heart

The river is whispering

Singing with me

About hopes and dreams

The fishes are always happy

Do not understand the desolation of walkers

They spit out a string of bubbles

Just like my dream

It's just the splendor of the meteors

The persistent footsteps

Run towards the destination of heart

Without any hesitation

Despite too many fetters

孤独之恋

与影相伴
倾听心灵的呼唤
无需言语
已泪水涟涟
多少无眠的夜晚
命运之神
带着妖媚的面具
我看不清方向
迷路在孤独的森林
发现一棵快乐的小草
顺着风的方向
我看到了朝阳
与朝阳为伴
让森林消失在遥远的昨天

The Love of Loneliness

Accompanied by my shadow

I listen to the voice of mind

No need for words

I have already been tearful

In many sleepless nights

The god of fate

Wears a seductive mask

I can't see the directions

Getting lost in the lonely forests

I find a happy grass

Following the wind

I see the rising sun

And keep it company

Let the forest disappear in the remote past

文之至妙
夜之灿阳

Chapter Five

Wonderful Words,
Bright Sun of Night

青春墨迹

青春的记忆
始于第一次握住钢笔的兴奋与新奇
希望能在作业本上写下漂亮的字
能够看到老师微笑的赞许和父母眼中的希冀
心中总有不竭的动力

青春的记忆
写满一篇篇长长短短的日记
记录着成长的欢乐与悲喜
每一页都是珍贵的故事
像花园里盛开的蔷薇

青春的记忆
深藏于一首首青涩的诗
讲述着一个女孩紫色的心事
翱翔天际的豪迈抑或坠入深海的低迷
都是生活的慷慨赠予

青春的记忆
缘于对文字的痴迷
那恣意挥洒的畅快淋漓
那尤具美感的工整韵律
胜过所有丹青好手的卓然技艺

我的青春
用笔刻下岁月的痕迹
苦涩的 快慰的 感动的
筑成一面斑驳的墙壁
为我的灵魂遮风挡雨

我的青春
有蒲公英的勇敢无惧
有银杏的挺拔坚持
还有凤凰花的热烈绚丽
每一种轮廓都有着傲然的风姿

只此一次的青春
犹如焰火般璀璨无比
亦如昙花般稍纵即逝
每每忆起让心房柔软的青春
总会有光芒跃出眼底
却在开口时欲言又止

只此一次的青春
文字是最鲜明的印迹
年少的懵懂 跋涉的伤痛
——用笔镌刻
打造属于自己的青春丰碑
散落于季节里星星点点的墨迹
是对青春时光的献礼
是对自由灵魂的疼惜
是一株用汗水与泪滴浇灌的馨香茉莉
它将永远与我相依

青春的墨迹
如晨露无瑕晶莹
似眼眸清澈明净
青春的墨迹
让未来的光阴
得以在繁华和荒芜中安然栖息

The Writing of Youth

The memory of youth

Begins with the excitement and novelty of holding a pen for the first time

I hope to write pretty characters in the exercise book

I can see the praise of teachers and the expectations in parents' eyes

I always have an inexhaustible motive force in my heart

The memory of youth

Is written in the long and short diaries

Recording the happiness and sadness of growing up

Every page is a precious story

Like a rose in the garden

The memory of youth

Deeply hides in the immature poems

Telling the purple mind of a girl

Either the boldness of soaring in the sky or the depress of falling into the deep sea

Is the gift from life

第五篇章

文之至妙

夜之灿阳

The memory of youth

Originates from the obsession with words

Writing freely and delightfully

Together with the aesthetic orderly rhythm

Outmatches all painters' skills

My youth

Carves the traces of time with pen

The bitter, the pleasant or the moving

All built into a mottled wall

Sheltering my soul from the wind and rain

My youth

Has the bravery of dandelion

And possesses the insistence of ginkgo

Together with the warmness of flamboyant flower

Each outline has an air of pride

The youth for once

Resplendent like fireworks

Fleeting like the epiphyllum

Whenever I recall my youth that pulls at my heartstrings

There is always light leaping out of my eyes

But I become silent when words are on the tip of my tongue

The youth for once

With words being the most striking signs

The ignorance of young age and the pains of treks

Both are carved by pen

To craft my own youth monument

The signs scattered in seasons

Are a gift presented to youth time

The empathy for free soul

The fragrant jasmine watered with sweat and tears

Will always be here with me

The signs of youth

Are like the flawless and translucent morning dew

And the pure eyes

The signs of youth

Makes the future time

Peacefully live in the prosperity and desolation

第五篇章

文之至妙

夜之灿阳

声为双翼文翩然

文字是生命的敏锐触角

发现惊喜与美好

亦倾诉失落与烦恼

抒家国情怀之深切

亦表人生况味之交叠

赏文者以声诵之

声情皆合

辅以腔圆顿挫

佳文顿似生出双翼

翩飞入怀

如此这般神思萦绕

即为诵读之悦

声绎之妙

Lively Writing Works With Voice as Wings

The words are the sensitive feeler of life

They discover surprise and beauty

Also pour out loss and annoyance

They expressing deep patriotic feelings

Also express various tastes of life

Appreciate the articles with recitation

Voice and emotion match

With standard pronunciation and orderly pause

The excellent articles seem to have two wings

Flying into the arms

Such sound lingering

Is the joy of recitation

And the beauty of sound deduction

第五篇章

文之至妙 夜之灿阳

诗之恋

诗
流淌出生命的力量
动听你我的惆怅
每一个音符
都是峥嵘岁月的模样
或许沧桑
却真实地让人无法遗忘
记于纸上
刻在心房
让往事随风徜徉
无法抵抗
那些曾经的忧伤
生命继续延长
我们不再躲藏
欣然面对
无论朗朗月光
抑或黯然神伤

都用诗

用诗一样的颜色

用诗一样的眼光

将一切

点亮

第五篇章　文之至妙　夜之灿阳

The Love of Poetry

The poetry

Flows out the power of life

Make melancholy become tuneful

Each note

Mirrors the eventful years

Maybe it is mostly vicissitudes

But it is truly unforgettable

Write it down on paper

Engrave it in the heart

Let the past swing with the wind

It is unable to resist

Those once sorrows

Life continues to extend

We no longer hide

But face it cheerfully

Whether it is the bright moon

Or the sadness

With the help of poetry

With poetic colors

With poetic eyes

Make everything

Lighten up

第五篇章　文之至妙　夜之灿阳

那一朵百合

踮起脚

我要那朵微笑的百合

哦，她在笑

欢乐如期而至

我来不及藏匿

拿一本诗集

将她高高托起

那是纯洁的赞美啊

发自紫色的心房

永不凋零吧

百合

我愿用滴血的青春交换

The Lily

Standing on my tiptoe

I want the smiling lily

Oh she is smiling

Joy is coming

I have no time to hide

Using a book of poetry

I lift her up high

That's the pure praise

From purple heart

Never wither

Lily

I'm willing to exchange with my most precious youth

第五篇章　文之至妙　夜之灿阳

甘苦况味绣行囊

咸涩的泪
是灵魂的甘露
滋润枯槁的心
让我品尝深藏于沧桑中的香醇绵长

清晨的阳
是希望的曙光
照亮一切晦暗
让我燃起跋涉的渴望

手中的笔
是梦想的长矛
刺醒慵懒的灵魂
让我与文字相拥舞蹈

最不能忘
那闪烁泪光
让双眼穿透迷雾
还给我最初坚强

过往忧伤

如光影般变幻登场

前行的双腿

铅一般沉重沮丧

或许还会遇见不幸与灾荒

我向每一处荆棘致谢

更向一场场暴雨微笑

是你们让一个旅人欣赏到绝美风光

是你们让步伐更有力量

我从不贪图赐予的华衣彩裳

唯有那险峰的奇峻

还有那孤独中的狂喜

让我向往

出发吧

带上晨风的歌唱

背起时光的行囊

脚下的路正追随我眺望的眼光

咸涩的泪

在曙光中告别忧伤

手中的笔

亲吻岁月诗行

未来的谜底

是彩虹的模样

Joys and Sorrows Embroider the
Luggage of Time

The bitter tears

Are the sweet dew of soul

Moistens the withered heart

Let me taste the fragrance hidden in the vicissitudes

The morning sun

Is the dawn of hope

Lights up all the darkness

Triggers my desire to trek

The pen in hand

Is the spear of dream

Wakes up the lazy soul

Lets me dance with words

The most unforgettable

Are the twinkling tears

They let me see through the mist

Bring back my original strength

The past sorrows

Appear on the stage like the light and shade

Legs going forward

Are heavy and depressed as lead

Perhaps there will be misfortune and famine

I thank every thorn

Smile to each storm

It's you let a traveler admire the beautiful scenery

It's you who make the pace stronger

I never covet the given finery

Only the precipitousness of dangerous peaks

And the ecstasy within loneliness

Stimulates my yearning

Let's start off

Bring the songs of morning breeze

Carry the luggage of time

The road under my feet is following my sight forward

第五篇章

文之至妙 夜之灿阳

The bitter tears

Leave the sadness in the dawn

The pen in my hand

Kisses the poem of time

The answer of future

Is the rainbow scene

悦夜

静谧冬夜

耳边唯有城市浅浅的鼻息

偶尔疾驰的铁骑

是她梦中的呓语

没有了温暖时节的蛙声虫鸣

世界就是巨幅的丹青墨品

如此画中佳境

怎会令人感到一丝寒意

手持香茗独饮

轻酌数盏已然略带醉意

最爱这静夜的丰富旖旎

犹如欣赏最美的文字

白昼的喧嚣知趣地逃离

畏惧这易辨真伪的安宁

天地于此刻回归远古的初始

只有那映照着高脚杯的彩色霓虹

标榜着繁华的印记

凭栏远眺

星星点点的灯火是这座夜城的眼睛

与天宇闪烁的繁星默契辉映
它们一定在分享各自的精彩故事
也交换着彼此最深的心事
我不忍打扰这群可爱的精灵
轻轻闭上双眼
去约会那颗早已久候的星

The Joyful Night

In the quiet winter night

I only can hear the breath of the city

Occasional speeding car

Is her talk in dream

Without the sound of the frog singing in warm season

The world is a huge ink–painting

Such a beautiful picture

Surprisingly gives me a chill

Drink the tea alone

Several cups already make me slightly drunk

I love this beautiful and silent night

Just like enjoying the most wonderful words

The bustle of the day escapes sensibly

I fear the peace that can tell the truth from the false

Heaven and earth return to ancient times at this moment

Only the colorful neon lights illuminate the tall glasses

Flaunting the prosperous imprint

Overlook from the balustrade

Tiny spots of lights are the eyes of this night city

第五篇章

文之至妙 夜之灿阳

With the stars sparkling in the sky

They must be sharing their own wonderful stories

And exchanging their deepest feelings

I can't bear to disturb these lovely spirits

And close my eyes gently

To date the star that has long been waiting for me

远方的灵魂

——怀念汪国真先生

当青春的手中不再握着香甜的冰淇淋
纯真的笑容躲进带锁的日记
原本在风中欢唱的风筝
被细雨淋湿

一位诗人拿起素笔
讲述白衣少年的心事
用诗句将远方融入青春的热血
当伙伴们渐渐离去
往日的嬉戏变成伤感的回忆
青春的心房变得荒芜凄清
一位诗人为年轻的骑士摇动旌旗
将孤独定格为青春的流星
跳动的心不再惧怕孤旅
从此执着笃定

什么样的语言能够放飞眼中的希冀
那一定是来自山巅的雄鹰
曾拥有搏击长空的旅行
那一定是来自远方的目光
深邃而宽广
成为前行的航标
为年轻的心终结无助与绝望
如此深沃营养
让跋涉与攀登总伴着轻舞飞扬
纵使前路充满未知与迷茫
亦有笔下清泉将双眸的尘埃涤荡

这就是一位诗人的光芒
拨开迷雾与阴霾
驱走黑暗与忧伤
让青春的肩膀背上温暖的行囊
当行至时光的尽头
再次回首曾经的脆弱与彷徨
将深深庆幸在向日葵盛开的时节
与一朵绽放在远方的灵魂邂逅
自此永不诀别

Distant Soul

——In Memory of Mr. Wang Guozhen

When the hands of youth no longer hold sweet ice cream

The pure smiles hide in a locked diary

The kite singing in the wind

Wetted by drizzle

A poet picked up a plain pen

To tell the thoughts of the boy in white

To blend the distance into the blood of youth with poems

When the friends drift away

Past enjoyment has become a sad memory

The heart of youth became desolation

A poet waved the flags for the young knights

To set loneliness as a meteor of youth

The beating hearts no longer fear the lonely trip

From then on they are persistently determined

第五篇章

文之至妙 夜之灿阳

162

What langue can fly the hope in eyes

It must be the eagle from the top of the mountain

That once traveled and fought in the sky

It must be a distant view

Deep and broad

To be the navigation mark

Ending helplessness and despair for young hearts

Such rich nutrition

Lets trekking and climbing always be with light dance

Though future is full of unknown and confusion

There is still the clear spring from the pen cleaning the dust

in the eyes

This is the light of a poet

He dispelled fog and haze

Drove away darkness and sorrow

Let the shoulder of youth carry the warm luggage

When reaching the end of time

Look back at the fragility and hesitation once again

We will be deeply grateful in the season of sunflowers

For meeting a soul blooming in the distance

We will never separate from now on

栖心

如果生命是一场旅行

我选择辛劳的攀登

尽管举步维艰

却能拥有未知风景带来的惊喜无限

如果生命是一条漫长的路

我选择坎坷之径

尽管满程荆棘

却能留下看似蹒跚实为清晰深刻的印迹

如果生命是一幅画卷

我选择青青翠竹

尽管没有色彩妖娆

却镌刻着心底那份永恒的灵魂相依

人生总有不期而至的仁慈与温暖

让时光温润而柔软

属于我的巍峨山峰

尽管险峻崎岖

却一路花香与奇遇

慰藉一颗勇敢纯净的心

那条延伸至天际的曲折路

尽管刺痛双足

亦有欢歌雀跃的坦途

消散一份源自深山晨露的孤独

我钟爱的那帧丹青

尽管只是写意的一抹绿

却在我眼中绽放着永不凋零的花期

生命的流年没有假设

唯有用忙碌与付出编织出无悔时刻

我不曾苛求生活

惟愿在每个唯一的分秒

营养渐次丰盈的羽毛

当风雪肆虐欺凌

我当挺身抗击

如此不负光阴

见证命运与时光的传奇

或许

能有幸邂逅一幅画 一条路 一座峰

我将用飞行的轨迹勾勒岁月的掠影

Habitat of My Heart

If the life is a journey

I choose the arduous climbing

Despite the difficulties

I will gain infinite surprises brought by unknown scenery

If the life is a long road

I choose the rough one

Though it is full of thorns

I will leave a tottering but clear, deep trace

If the life is a picture

I choose the green bamboos

Although they lack enchanting colors

They engrave the eternal soul on the bottom of my heart

Life is full of unexpected kindness and warmth

That make the time soft and tender

On the towering mountains of my own

Although roads are steep and rough

There are flower fragrance and adventures

Comforting a brave and pure heart

On the tortuous road extending to the horizon

第五篇章

文之至妙 夜之灿阳

Although it stings my feet

There are also joyful and smooth parts

That dissipate loneliness from a deep mountain morning dew

My favorite ink painting wash

Is just a touch of green

But in my eyes it's a never–withered flower

There is no assumption about the fleeting time of life

Only diligence and devotion can make fulfilling moments

I never demand excessively from life

Only wish every moment

Can give nutrition to my increasingly fledged feathers

When the wind and snow rage

I will stand up and fight

So my days will not pass in vain

I will witness the legend of fate and time

What if

I'm lucky enough to come across a picture, a road, or a mountain

I will outline the years with my track of flight

季之永迭

眸之恒悦

Chapter Six

Ever-changing Seasons,
Eternally Joyful Eyes

季之悠怀

当蝉的交响化作流年的光影
秋叶开始伴着苍凉飘零
翩然一舞
便开启绝世孤独
何其悲壮
不忍伫赏
此刻不禁痛怀早春
一如怀念镜中的明眸青丝
那是时光的乳牙
季节的白塔
有小草与枝头的热闹竞发
还有河水池塘的新奇喧哗
于是喟叹在桃花相映时
没能留住那抹最美的霞
为何这般
眼前之景总引伤怀
心中之念又常伴无奈

此般愁思

终让含苞的蕾浸透咸涩泪海

何不将时光的刺化为铠甲

抵挡前行的冰雹与风沙

纵遇凛冽寒冬

嘶吼到沙哑

依然战衣披挂

与荆棘宿敌果勇厮杀

The Feelings of Seasons

When the cicadas'symphony fades away as the light and shadow

of the fleeting year

Autumn leaves fall down with desolation

Lightly a dance

Starts its great loneliness in the world

How tragically heroic they are

That I can't bear to stand and appreciate

I can't help missing the early spring

As I miss the bright eyes and black hair in the mirror

That is the time's baby teeth

The white pagoda of the season

There is a lively competition between grass and branches

And the fresh and curious roar of rivers and ponds

The sigh when peach blossoms are in bloom

Fail to keep the most beautiful rosy clouds

Why it's always the case

That I get sentimental over the view before my eyes

That I feel helpless over the thought in my mind

Such melancholy

Will soak the buds into the sea of salty tears

Why not turn the thorn of time into armor

To resist the hail and sandstorm forward

Despite the cold winter

Until I shout myself hoarse

I will still be in my armor

And fight bravely in thorns against enemies

第六篇章　季之永迭　眸之恒悦

季节恋人

当温润的春风唤醒沉睡的冬叶

我向枝头的新绿微笑

感谢季节赐予希望的幼苗

当夏日的热浪席卷赤裸的大地

飘飞的裙裾与胸中的火焰一同燃烧

当秋雨打湿沉默的屋檐

我看见风铃快乐地舞蹈

那悦动的节拍是丰收的讯号

当刺骨的寒风将最后一只松鼠赶入树洞

我将收获缝进厚厚的衣角

身后一串串坚定的脚印记录着一年的骄傲

季节的耳朵听不到都市的喧嚣

也从不理会世人的争吵

它伴随着潮汐的心情

和着月亮的步调

将时光涂上缤纷的颜料

季节转身

我们悄然苍老

镜中的华发

诉说着岁月中无数次的奋进与跌倒

或许我们应该放慢脚步

静享一段柔软的时光

把儿时的纯真嵌入睫毛

以轩然的姿态

走过年轮里永不重复的每分每秒

在阴霾中心存阳光

在悲伤中回忆美好

在淡然中恋上季节的曼妙

期待丁香花与木棉相遇在早春的街角

在惊鸿中交换彼此的心跳

我听到黄鹂与蜗牛一起祈祷

它们希望再次见到弯弯的彩虹桥

与季节相恋

时光的尽头是星星与银河的拥抱

The Lover of Seasons

When the warm spring wind wakes up the sleeping winter leaves

I smile to the fresh green branches

Thanks to the season for the seedlings of hope

When the summer heat sweeps the naked earth

The flying skirt burns with the flame in the chest

When autumn rains wet silent eaves

I see the wind bells dancing happily

The happy beat is the signal of harvest

When the biting wind blows the last squirrel into the tree hole

I sew the harvest into the thick clothes

A string of firm footprints record the pride of the year

Season's ears can't hear the noise of the city

And never care the quarrels of the world

It accompanies the mood of the tide

With the paces of moon

Paint the time with colorful pigment

Seasons alternate

We grow old quietly

The white hair in the mirror

Tells countless progress and fall in past years

Maybe we should slow down

Enjoy a soft time quietly

Embed childhood innocence into eyelashes

With an imposing manner

Live every minute and second that never repeat

Keep the sunshine in heart when passing through the haze

Recall the good memories when in sorrow

Love the graceful seasons with detached mind

Expect lilac and kapok to meet at the corner in early spring

Exchange each other's heartbeat in a fleeting glimpse

I hear the oriole and the snail pray together

They hope to see the curved rainbow bridge again

Love with seasons

The end of time is the embrace of stars and the Milky Way

第六篇章 季之永迭 眸之恒悦

春耘

这个春天

温润的气息让枯枝找回童年

最是那一抹新绿

点亮一双双黑夜中跋涉的眼

塘边的柳絮

随风蹁跹

享受着与春风约会的时间

这份季节的恩赐

胜过无数期许的诺言

深藏许久的心芽

在此刻破土萌发

震颤着满树欣喜的枝桠

于是

微笑着端详世界

当目光投向田野

农人们正用咸涩的汗水种下青翠的秧苗

眼里企盼着秋的金黄

放眼一所所可爱的学校

课堂上是求知的渴望与书声朗朗

少年们用寒窗岁月靠近梦想的远方

当目光定格于座座高楼

人们正用忙碌的节奏诉说青春的追求

或许这就是春的光影拼图

花红柳绿的光阴不适合蹉跎虚度

而应以新生的勇气开启又一个年轮的序幕

无论你的土地肥沃还是贫瘠

耕耘的光阴都会生长出甘甜的果实

这是季节对春的回报

更是时光对劳作的犒赏

不曾止步的心跳经营着青春的梦工厂

当大雁南飞银杏金黄

你的眼眸

将闪动着麦浪的光芒

Ploughing in Spring

This spring

Moist breath makes dry branches find their childhood

It's the new green

Lights up pairs of eyes in the dark night

The catkins by the pond

Are dancing with the wind

Enjoying the dating time with spring breeze

This gift of the season

Better than numerous expected promises

Heart bud hiding for a long time

Is breaking the soil and sprouting at this moment

The branches tremble with joy

Thereupon

Looking at the world with a smile

Eyes on the field

Farmers are planting green seedlings with salty sweat

The eyes expect the golden autumn

Looking at lovely schools

In class are the thirst for knowledge and the sound of reading aloud

Teenagers are approaching the distance of dreams with persistent study

When the eyes are fixed on tall buildings

People are telling the pursuit of youth with busy rhythm

Maybe this is the light and shadow puzzle of spring

The time of vitality is not suitable for idling

We should start another year with new courage

Whether your land is rich or poor

Ploughing time will produce sweet fruits

This is the reward from seasons to spring

From time to hard work

The incessant heartbeat runs the DreamWorks of youth

When the wild geese fly south and ginkgoes are golden

Your eyes

Will be shining with the light of wheat wave

第六篇章 季之永迭 眸之恒悦

春翼翔

眼中的黎明

涂着岁月的晶莹

一江碧水

映出如火的朝阳

我的快乐也冉冉升起

升起在盎然的春季

温柔的柳枝诉说着翠绿的欣喜

小草也挥洒着生命的豪情

与孩子们一起嬉戏

展示着历经严寒后的生机

我穿着美丽的衣裳

与春天一起歌唱

沐浴着春光

心儿不再流浪

远处有飞鸟仍在翱翔

我会飞得更远更高

因为我有一双爱的翅膀

为你远航

越过山岗

越过蓝色海洋

在春天

奏一曲爱的乐章

第六篇章　季之永迭　眸之恒悦

Wings of Spring

The dawn in eyes

Is painted with years of sparkle

A river of clear water

Is reflecting the rising sun

My happiness is also rising

Rising in the exuberant spring

The tender willow branches tell the green joy

Grass also sprinkles the passion of life

They play with the children

Showing the vitality after the bitter cold

I am wearing beautiful clothes

Singing with the spring

Bathed in spring light

My heart is no longer wandering

There are birds still flying in the distance

I can fly farther and higher

Because I have wings of love

Sailing for you

Crossing hills

Across the blue ocean

In spring

Play a movement of love

第六篇章　季之永迭　眸之恒悦

春之悦盼

杨柳堤岸

风舞蝶欢

枝条摇曳春的期盼

最是那青草依依

铺就一张张高贵的绿毡

牵牛花不敢笑出声

只用力地将小喇叭吹成一个满圆

我在画中行走

欢喜的心跳勾画出蜿蜒的湖畔

垂柳含笑

对镜梳妆

将自己打扮成春的新娘

桃花不语

在枝头妩媚

将笑靥映入踏青人的眼眸

最是那含苞的花蕾

难掩动人娇羞

怯生生地望着一切

幻想着绽放的瑰丽

我倚着高高的木棉

凝望着那一朵朵醉人的红

深深呼吸着浓郁的芬芳

脑海中依稀掠过冬的严酷

仿佛还见几片无奈的枯黄

庆幸正身处这温暖之季

此刻

裙裾翻飞

让心带着绿色的梦

随柔软春风

飘向遥远

Joyful Expectation of Spring

On the willow bank

Butterflies dance in the wind

Twigs are swaying the expectation of spring

You see the green grass

Spread out the noble carpets

Morning glory flower dare not laugh

It just blows the trumpet into a full circle

I walk in the picture

My joyful heartbeat outlines the winding lakeside

Weeping willow with smile

Is dressing up in front of the mirror

To be the bride of spring

Peach blossoms do not speak

They are showing their charms on the branches

Their smiling faces are in the eyes of spring sightseers

The tender buds

Can not conceal their shy charms

And look at everything with fear

Imagining the magnificent blooms

I lean on the tall kapok tree

Staring at the intoxicating red flowers

I deeply breathe in rich fragrance

The bitter winter appears in my mind

I seemingly see a few helpless yellow leaves

I am glad to be in this warm season

At this moment

Skirt is flying

Let the heart bring a green dream

Following the soft spring breeze

And float far away

第六篇章　季之永迭　眸之恒悦

夏之炽焰

烈日点燃了蝉的翅膀

它高声呐喊不再飞翔

刻板的沥青路面

也变得柔软滚烫

不息的车流带走了它的慌张

最是那绽放的石榴

早已被烤得花了妆容

娇嗔地低眉含羞

每一丝呼吸都张扬着夏的威力

这个以炽热著称的季节

将一切变得明艳热烈

像极了艺术家眼中的执着

追逐之光永不熄灭

这团天空赐予的火

在夜色中倔强告别

与旭日相伴而跃

续写属于火焰的章节

Blazing Flames of Summer

The hot sun lights the wings of cicadas

They shout loudly but no longer fly

The stiff asphalt pavement

Becomes soft and hot

The incessant traffic flow takes away its panic

The blooming pomegranate

Has its makeup destroyed by the heat

With a low brow and shyness

Every breath shows the power of summer

This season is known for its blazing heat

It makes everything bright and hot

Like the persistence in the eyes of artists

The light of pursuit never goes out

The fire from the sky

Makes a stubborn farewell in the night

With the rising sun

It continues to write chapters that belong to fire

第六篇章　季之永迭　眸之恒悦

秋之盈硕

当冰淇淋躲进童话的城堡
树叶披上了诱人的金黄
田里的稻子已经笑弯了腰
它们要给劳作的人们最好的回报
那是与春天呼应的符号
那是对耕耘最大的犒劳
秋天在镰刀的挥舞中长高
在落叶的旋转中微笑
丰收是这个季节亮眼的曲调
是汗水折射出的骄傲
拥着秋风起舞
你将听到一粒种子的歌谣

Abundance of Autumn

When ice cream hides in the castle of fairy tales

The leaves were clothed with attractive gold

The rice plants in the field have become bent with laughter

They want to give the best reward to the laboring people

That is the symbol of echo to spring

That's the biggest reward for ploughing

Autumn grows high in the swing of sickle

It smiles in the rotation of fallen leaves

Harvest is a bright tune in this season

It's the pride reflected by sweat

Dancing with the autumn wind

You will hear the song of a seed

第六篇章　季之永迭　眸之恒悦

冬之净素

转动季节的风车
岁月的衣衫五光十色
路过葱茏与炽热
告别深沉与丰硕
迎来净素与萧瑟
冷峻的冬藏起时光的皱褶
清寒的风中
心事竖起衣领
丰盈一秋的田野
土地平静地重温着喜悦
往日的一树繁花
独留枝干望尽天涯
冬的气质
犹如时光之蚌孕育的珍珠
那沉淀后的净润通透
分明就是雪冬的明眸

Clean and Simple Winter

Turning the windmill of seasons

The clothes of time have a great variety of colors

Passing through verdure and heat

Leaving depth and harvest

Here comes the season of simplicity and desolation

The cold winter hides the wrinkles of time

In the cold wind

The thoughts put up the collar

The field had abundant crops during the whole autumn

The land is quietly reliving its joy

A tree had numerous flowers in the past

While the branches are left alone to see the end of the world

The temperament of winter

Is like the pearl bred by the clam of time

The pure and transparent properties after precipitation

Are clearly the bright eyes of snowing winter

193

第六篇章 季之永迭 眸之恒悦

第七篇章

抱之以诚
付之以真

Chapter Seven

Insistence on Sincerity,
Devotion to Truth

这一天，心房闪耀

鹭岛时光
柔软绵长
徜徉在贝壳的乐园
咸涩的海风冷冷地告诉我
我在异乡

漫步湖畔
满目丰盈
那坚强的木棉
依然红硕端庄
一张张陌生的脸孔漠然地提醒我
我在流浪

游走街巷
任思绪被强行拉长
一扇扇橱窗
炫耀着琳琅满日的张狂
那似笑非笑的衣架模特
看穿了我的忧伤

如此穿梭在时光的缝隙
眼神犹如叶子的脉络
简单而透着些许神秘
这一天
惊喜而现
让我在云端欢欣舞蹈

久违的感动
默契地齐集而至
黯然的心雀跃欢动
原来我的世界不只是荒芜苍凉
也有温暖星光

来自远方的牵挂
是一朵晶莹剔透的花
让黑白岁月瞬增缤纷
含泪感恩
泣谢挚爱亲友
让一颗些许冷却的心重获暖意

挥别惆怅
将美好珍藏
嘴角微扬
欣然面对一向敬畏的时光

起身伫立
窗外是一群即将告别校园的学子
与红色祥云般的凤凰花一同欢笑
用镜头将青春定格

我用诗行将岁月定格
当一切尘封久远
那些值得珍藏的记忆
依然鲜活闪耀

The Heart Shines on This Day

The time on Xiamen Island

Is soft and long

Wandering in the paradise of shells

I am told by the salty sea breeze coldly

I am in a strange land

I stroll along the lake

Things are in abundance

The strong kapok trees

Are still red and elegant

Strange faces remind me indifferently

I am wandering

Walking on the streets

Let my thoughts be forcibly lengthened

The show windows

Are madly showing the collection of beautiful things

The dummy with a faint smile on its face

Sees through my sadness

第七篇章

抱之以诚

付之以真

Shuttling in the gap of time

My eyes are like the veins of leaves

Simple and mysterious

This day

Surprise appears

And let me dance on the clouds

Long—lost touched feelings

Come together tacitly

Gloomy heart becomes full of joy

My world is not just desolation

There is also the warm starlight

Care from afar

Is a crystal clear flower

It makes the black and white days colorful immediately

Grateful with tears

I thank my beloved relatives and friends

For letting a cooling heart warm again

Quit melancholy

Treasure the beauties

Slightly smile

Gladly face the time of which I stood in awe

Stand up gently

Outside the window are students who are going to leave the
campus

Laughing with the flamboyant flowers that are like red clouds

They use cameras to capture youth

I use poetry to capture time

When everything long become past

The memories worth cherishing

Are still alive and shining

第
七
篇
章

抱
之
以
诚

付
之
以
真

荒漠花语

当光阴的脚步被城市追赶

当鸟儿的天堂被高楼侵占

曾经悦耳的歌声变成无声的呐喊

残存的几分绿意

勉强保持着季节的习惯

如此灰色布景

如何演绎春的缤纷绚烂

难道那一袭袭飘飞的裙裾

和一盏盏霓虹的阑珊

就是如今季节的流转

路旁的花草传达着城市的绿色理念

可却默默承受终日的轰鸣与车流的硝烟

花儿们多希望自己生长在山林或乡间

即使无人欣赏赞叹

却能畅快呼吸每一秒的新鲜

每当凝望风中的花草

总想为她们抵挡尘世的喧嚣

让每一片花瓣都拥有舒心的微笑

或许在如此周遭中成长

唯有选择如沙漠玫瑰般桀骜坚强

没有终年的雨露滋润

亦没有时时的呵护照料

一样热情燃烧

一样淋漓绽放

在无垠荒漠中

以怒放的姿态

坦然面对无数惊异目光

那摇曳生姿的花叶

独自承受所有悲伤与喜悦

她笃定地坚守着自己的花期与时节

只为那等候千年的惊鸿一瞥

The Monologue of Desert Rose

When the flow of time is outpaced by the city

When the paradise of birds is occupied by the skyscrapers

The once melodious songs fade into a silent cry

Some remaining green

Barely keeps the normalcy of seasons

How can such gray settings

Depict the colorful spring

Are the skirts swinging in the wind

Together with the glaring neon lights

Indicating the turn of seasons

The flowers and plants on the roadside convey the green concept

of the city

But silently bear the roar and exhaust of traffic flow all day

How they wish to grow in the mountains and countryside

Even without any appreciation or admiration

Yet they can heartily breathe the fresh air

Whenever I gaze at the flowers and plants in the wind

Always do I want to filter out the hustle and bustle for them

Let every petal have a pleasant smile

Maybe growing in such an environment

The only choice is to be strong like a desert rose

Even without year-round rain or dew

Or all-time concern and care

It still burns passionately

Still blooms thoroughly

In the boundless desert

In a manner of full bloom

It frankly faces countless astonished eyes

The swaying flowers and leaves

Bear alone all the joy and sadness

She sticks firmly to her florescence and season

Just for an amazing glimpse that has been waiting for a thousand

years

第七篇章

抱之以诚　付之以真

心事茶蘼

寂寞窗台

长满爬山虎的关爱

层层绿意

在风中无尽开怀

屋角的蔷薇独自盛开

似清丽女子站在无人舞台

花瓣玲珑

含羞等待

你英眉微蹙

我陷入忧伤的海

你说爱情的花期在夏季

却转身错过了那场最美的雨

我仍在原地

拥抱的姿势依然清晰

只是已没有人入戏

白纱的窗台

将心事藏入花海

它在怒放时澎湃

在凋谢时醒来

请打开我送你的信笺

微笑着看完荼靡花事的对白

第七篇章 抱之以诚 付之以真

The Thought of Heart Blooming

The lonely windowsill

Is covered by loving Boston ivies

Layers of green

Show endless joy in the wind

The rose in the corner is blooming on its own

Like a beautiful girl standing on an stage alone

The petals are exquisite

Waiting shyly

You frown lightly

I fall into a sea of sadness

You said the bloom of love is in summer

But turned around and missed the most beautiful rain

I'm still here

The gesture of embrace is still clear

But no one else has entered the drama

Windowsill with white screen

Hides its mind in flowers

It surges in full bloom

Wakes up in the withering

Please open the letter I sent you

Smile after watching the dialogue of the flowers

第七篇章　抱之以诚　付之以真

为爱情命名

缘份默铭牵引

两颗心浪漫相遇

鸿雁遥传情意

我为你千里梦行

漂泊流浪的双翼

从此在幸福城堡远离风雨

你说平淡才是生活的本真

我却企盼激起青春的涟漪

时光在温情牵手中飞逝

天使降临是命运最好的恩赐

幸福城堡从此增添盎然生机

你说爱情就是孩子成长的脚印

我常常凝望那写满童真的眼睛

总想用心爱的文字为我的爱情命名

却笨拙地描绘不出半幅风景

也许一切早已烙上亲情的印记

我的心

像停在半空的画笔

细细品味平凡的点滴

才发现每个清晨和日暮都有最纯美的回忆

我不再渴求如昙花盛开般绚烂的奇迹

只留下岁月洗礼后的平静与安宁

此刻我手中的笔

饱蘸爱的墨汁

在纸上坚定前行

走向幸福最深处

那里一定有桃源仙境

繁花似锦

Naming My Love

Fate is a wonderful guide

Two hearts meet romantically

Letters convey distant affection

I went thousands of miles for you

The wandering wings

From then on nestle in the happy castle away from the wind and rain

You said simplicity is the essence of life

But I hoped to stir up the ripples of youth

Time flies in the tender love

Angel is the best gift of fate

The castle of happiness is full of vitality since then

You say love is the footprints of kid's growth

I often gaze at the eyes full of childlike innocence

I always want to use my beloved words to name my love

But I clumsily cannot describe half the scenery

Maybe everything has been branded with the mark of family love

My heart

Like a pen in the air

Is savoring every bit of ordinary things

I found that every morning and evening has the pure memories

I no longer long for the miracle like Epiphyllum blooming

Leaving only the peace and tranquility after the trails of the years

The pen in my hand at the moment

Full of ink of love

Is moving forward firmly on paper

Toward the depth of happiness

There must be a fairyland

Full of beautiful flowers

第
七
篇
章

抱
之
以
诚

付
之
以
真

凉夜

月光下

一杯苦丁茶

黑白岁月仿佛沙漏

从指间滑落

一壶浊酒

挥洒出古人的豪情

大江东去 晓风残月啊

都是人生的迷人恋曲

一如今夜的万家灯火

映照出人间的悲欢无数

疲倦的行人啊

跋涉在回家的途中

手里紧紧握着

那串开启幸福的钥匙

Cool Night

In the moonlight

A cup of bitter tea

Black and white time is like the sand in an hourglass

Slipping from fingers

A pot of unfiltered wine

Shows the heroic feelings of the ancients

The mighty river flows eastward, morning breeze and lingering
moon

Are all charming songs of life

Just like the twinkling lights in myriad homes tonight

Reflecting the countless joys and sorrows of the world

The tired walkers

Trudge on the way home

Hold tightly in the hand

The keys to happiness

第七篇章

抱之以诚　付之以真

月圆独语

盈盈圆月

映照思念残缺

树影婆娑

万缕情丝闪躲

与清风起舞

飞旋出跃动脚步

捧一汪清泉

沁润干涸心田

我像贪婪的小孩

期盼儿时纯真的爱

夜色穿过霓虹

填满所有懵懂

美丽笑靥

融入温柔眼眸

迷人的酒窝

将欢喜

到处散落

Monologue on a Full Moon Night

The full moon

Reflects the lonely yearning

The dancing shadow of trees

The passion is awakening

Dancing with the breeze

Twirling around with jumping steps

I hold the clear spring water in hands

To moisten the dry heart

I'm like a greedy child

Expect the pure love in childhood

The night goes through the neon lights

Fill all ignorance

The beautiful smile

Merges into the gentle eyes

The charming dimple

Brings the joy

To many places

第七篇章

抱之以诚　付之以真

念如磐

时光亦有执念

永续匆忙

世间繁华激荡

难令其伫足回望

唯有那颗心芽萌发

让蒲公英也有了牵挂

一场狂奔天涯的远行

一次折翅无悔的飞翔

跌跌撞撞

累累重伤

从不哭泣

绝不返航

只为最初的纯粹与倔强

纵然孤灯苦影

也在暗夜集聚星光

在某个苍白晦暗的时刻

点亮疲惫却依然坚毅的心房

Firm Faith

Time also has its persistence

Always in a hurry

The world is bustling with prosperity

It's hard to stop and look back

Only the adorable bud of heart sprouts

Making dandelion concerned

A long journey to the corners of the earth

A wing–breaking flight without regrets

Stumbling along the road

With numerous wounds

Never cry

Never return

Only for the original purity and stubbornness

Even during the bitter time with lonely lamp

There are stars gathering at dark night

In a pale and gloomy moment

They light tired but still determined heart

第七篇章

抱之以诚

付之以真

星恋

夜色为城市披上轻柔曼纱

遮住无数疲惫脸颊

周遭静谧如悬挂墙上的吉他

只有星星不肯入梦

低声耳语说着情话

原来星星也会失眠

遗憾永远见不到白昼的地面

每当晨曦来临

只能收起一生的好奇

与大地互说再见

再次相见时

一切已然谢幕告安

因而星星总是奋力地眨眼

想将大地端详得真切完全

这份小小的心愿

幻化为持久爱恋

穿越时空与风雨

磐石般执着不变

大地并非无情

只是不忍星星知晓白昼的苦辣酸甜

总是呈现安然恬静的脸

没有奔波劳累

没有无奈卑微

大地喜欢星星永远快乐地飞

没有烦恼伤悲

没有失望泪水

如此才可心安

因而在彼此眼中

星星总是亲切高远

大地总是神秘新鲜

这于天幕间的爱恋

令世人感怀艳羡

当夜色渐渐褪去

你可看见天空中那双深情的眼

Love of Stars

The city is draped with soft veil by night

Covering countless tired cheeks

It's as quiet as a guitar hanging on the wall

Only stars do not want to sleep

Murmuring words of love

The stars are also sleepless

Regret never seeing the ground in daylight

When the dawn comes

They can only put away lifelong curiosity

Say goodbye to the earth

When they meet again

Everything has come to an end

So the stars always blink hard

Wanting to see the earth thoroughly

This little wish

Turns into a lasting love

Through time and space and wind and rain

It's persistent as rock

The earth is not merciless

It can't bear to expose daytime intricacy to stars

Always presents a calm and peaceful face

Without hustle or tiredness

Without helplessness or inferiority complex

The earth loves to see stars fly happily forever

Without worry or sadness

Without disappointment or tears

Only in this way can it feel at ease

So in each other's eyes

The stars are always kind and far away

The earth is always mysterious and fresh

The love across the sky and land

Makes all the people admire

When the night is fading

Can you see the affectionate eyes in the sky

第七篇章

抱之以诚

付之以真

226